MANHUNT IN QUEMADO

Nix was a gun-runner and a killer. He turned Angel's sidekick loose – naked and unarmed – into the Valley of Death. Nix promised to come after him some time. Angel's mission was to find his friend's killer – but history repeated itself, and it was Angel who was alone in the desert. The hunter became the hunted.

MANHUNT IN QUEMADO

MANHUNT IN QUEMADO

by

Daniel Rockfern

Dales Large Print Books
Long Preston, North Yorkshire,
BD23 4ND, England.

British Library Cataloguing in Publication Data.

Rockfern, Daniel
Manhunt in Quemado.

A catalogue record of this book is available from the British Library

ISBN 978-1-84262-667-2 pbk

First published in Great Britain 1976
Originally published in paperback as *Manhunt in Quemado* by Frederick H. Christian

Published in Large Print 2009 by arrangement with Robert Hale Ltd.

Dales Large Print is an imprint of Library Magna Books Ltd.

Printed and bound in Great Britain by
T.J. (International) Ltd., Cornwall, PL28 8RW

For
Laurence James
who's a lot more character than I could ever make him into.

ONE

Another mile.

Ernie Hecatt raised a hand to shield his eyes while he squinted up at the sun, cursing its blinding light. Two, maybe three o'clock, he thought. Steadily and monotonously and without any real awareness of what he was saying – or indeed, the fact that he was saying anything – Hecatt cursed the relentless sun, the pitiless desert, his blistered feet, and his burned and wounded body. The effort of doing so was an extra his depleted frame could not afford, and he slumped down on the burning sand, crying – without tears, for his body was already well into the terminal stages of dehydration – in futile rage at his own weakness. Then he thought of the man who had reduced him to this, and as the name formed in his mind, he spat it out as a curse.

'Angel!' he coughed, getting to his knees. 'Frank Angel!' he croaked, staggering upright. As if the very movement itself released some further strength from a reservoir his body did not know it possessed, Hecatt stumbled forward. Using everything that he had left, he headed for the white scar on the land which he could vaguely see up ahead. His vision was already blurring, and he knew he had no margin for error left. What he saw might be an arroyo. It might be a swathe of gypsum sand. It might be nothing more than an outcropping of mica. Or it might – just might – be a trail.

With shaking legs and reaching hands, Ernie Hecatt stumbled toward his goal. A mumble came from his frayed lips. It would have been meaningless to anyone listening, had there been anyone in the empty wilderness. But there were only the patient buzzards high in the brazen sky above the lurching figure. To Hecatt, however, the mumble was words, and the words were a goad that spurred him on. It was the name that he had spoken before.

'Frank Angel!' he muttered. 'God damn your soul to Hell!'

Two years earlier, Ernie Hecatt had been one of the richest men in the state of Texas. Although he rarely left it, he was known throughout the United States. Bigtime politicians and moneymen found it well worth while to journey to his palatially sprawling ranch thirty miles outside Uvalde, or to the oak-paneled offices on Texas Street in town. It was said that Hecatt had no more respect for the law than he had to have, and that wasn't a hell of a lot. But nobody had ever caught him with his pants down. He was known as 'the man with the Midas touch.' He knew everybody who was anybody, or seemed to, and what was even more awesome was that he also seemed to know exactly what they were up to, what deals they were into, how thinly their resources were spread, and who was in what with whom. He could break his rivals and he sometimes did, not only financially but physically. He was a liar and a thief and everyone knew it, but nobody had ever told him so, any more than anyone had ever said out loud that Hecatt made a lot of his money ferrying repeating rifles to the *Comancheros*, who in turn sold them to the marauding Comanch' and Kiowa. Nobody talked up because Ernie Hecatt was also a cold-blooded killer, one of the mean-streak kind who liked to gutshoot his victims. They said he was faster with a gun than even Wes Hardin. That might have been an exaggeration, of course, because it was doubtful if the man ever walked the face of the earth who could have outdrawn John Wesley Hardin in his prime. But if it was an exaggeration, it wasn't much of one, and certainly nothing like enough of one to make many men want to put it to the test. Ernie Hecatt had killed upward of half a dozen who'd tried. He even paid the cost of burying them decently. It was one of his vanities. He said the very least you could do for a man you'd sent to the Pearly Gates was to make sure someone dug a hole and put him in it. Besides, Hecatt would say with the grin of a hunting wolf, corpses tend to lower the tone of a town if they're left lying around. Macabre, maybe. But damned effective, as Hecatt knew.

There were three things he didn't let anyone mess with: his possessions, his reputation, and his money. Until Frank Angel turned up in Uvalde nobody had ever dared, but by the time Angel was through – and it didn't take him long – Hecatt was busted wide open. Angel found weak points nobody had ever dreamed could be there and leaned on them. He not only challenged Hecatt's domination of the area, he destroyed it. He exposed the trick that held Hecatt's finances together and wiped him out, everything. Angel faced Hecatt down on every front because he knew that at heart Hecatt was a fraud. He out-thought him, outmaneuvered him, out-foxed him, and finally exposed him. Tempted him into a fool's play, and when Hecatt fell for it, Angel busted him mercilessly. With a United States Marshal and a posse along as witnesses, Angel arrested Hecatt while Hecatt was personally handing over cases of Winchester '66 repeaters to Leon Alevantal, the *Comanchero* whose business was trading arms and armor with the Comanch'. With no place left on earth to go, Hecatt then did the dumbest thing he'd ever done: he went for the gun at his side. In front of all of them: Alevantal and his brigands, the U.S. Marshal, all of them. And Angel let him.

Angel let him get good and started before he even moved his hand. Hecatt had had bad dreams about that moment ever since. He played and replayed it over and over in his mind, tasting the same sick fear as he remembered Angel's hand blurring faster than he could see, coming up so fast with the gun that he, Hecatt, had simply frozen with fear, his own Remington still only half-way out of the holster. Pride had told him to pull the gun anyway, and die with his head up. The green thing in his belly had made him let go of the revolver butt as if it were red-hot.

From that moment he was through and he knew it. He put up no further fight, and they took him in. The trial, the weeks of humiliation as the law stripped him one by one of all his possessions dissolved into a half-remembered blur. They sentenced him to ten year's hard labor at Huntsville. It was equivalent to a death sentence and everyone knew it: there was a shocked silence even in that hardened courtroom. Hecatt had gone like a lamb, only half hearing the jeers of men who not six weeks earlier would have curried his slightest favor, indulged his pettiest whim. They took him in a wagon to Huntsville, and there, rolling about in that gritty wagon-bed beneath the basilisk stare of the shotgun-armed deputy-marshals, he had vowed to have his vengeance, to repay every slight, every jeer, every insult tenfold. And most of all, to very slowly kill Frank Angel, Special Investigator of the Department of Justice, the man who had brought him down.

Hecatt was a model prisoner during his first year, and eventually, in keeping with the then-current practice, he was hired out as one of a gang of prisoners who worked as laborers for a subcontractor who was building a stretch of road between Galveston and Nacogdoches. One day, Hecatt's pickax smashed in the skull of the dozing guard nearest him, and he had the fallen rifle before it hit the dirt. He dropped the second guard before that man truly realized what had happened, and then he lit out. He shot the legirons off and headed for open country, making the long march back.

If they came after him, he never heard them. He was hardened by his time in prison and powered by revenge. He lived off the land like a hunting wolf, working across the wide flat emptiness of Edwards Plateau toward his own *querencia*, and making good time until he ran into the trio of Comanch'. They ran off his horse and kept him pinned down in a buffalo wallow until most of his ammunition and all of his water was gone. In the course of that long, seemingly endless day and night, he killed one of the Indians and wounded another, which in any circumstances except Ernie Hecatt's might have been fair exchange for the hole in his left arm the third Comanche had put there with his smooth-bore. When the brassy blue Texas morning pushed back the shadows, the Indians were gone, leaving Hecatt alone in the emptiness, without a horse or water, his left arm shot to pieces just above the wrist, and no place to head except out. He had been walking ever since.

Now he saw that the whitish-gray scar he had picked out was indeed a track, and he gave a croak of relief as he stumbled out of the clawing chaparral into the open. It was just a rutted wagontrack, but in this wide wilderness it was like a huge sign advertising that help was not far away. If there was a track it led somewhere, came from somewhere else. It could be ten, twenty, thirty miles, but at either end there would be people, water, surcease from the punishment of the merciless sun.

He stood teetering on the edge of the track. Which way? Right, left, which would bring him soonest to deliverance?

Ernie Hecatt decided to go left, and started staggering along the rutted road. He managed maybe a mile, looking for all the world like some weird animated scare-crow that occasionally laughed, weakly and insanely. But he had been on borrowed time before he even saw the trail, and now his legs would carry him no further. He sagged, tottered, and fell again. The world spun in front of his eyes, and a red curtain misted out his foreshortened view of the clump of prickly pear a foot from his face. This time not even the name of the man he hated most in all the world, the man he had sworn to kill, could animate his wasted frame.

'Angel!' he croaked once.

Then the curtain in front of his eyes turned from red to black. He was still lying there, nine-tenths dead, when Victoria Stacey found him four hours later.

TWO

'No!' said the Attorney-General. 'And that's final.'

'Give me one good reason.' Angel said.

'I don't have to,' his boss replied with a faint smile. 'That's one of the nicer things about being Attorney-General.'

'All right,' Angel said. 'You don't have to. But give me one anyway. That's the least you could do.'

'You'd be somewhat surprised at what the least I can do actually is,' the older man grinned. He was enjoying this tennis match of words, and his normally austere face was set in an untypically smiling expression this Fall day. Outside his windows the drizzle fell relentlessly down upon the muddy mess of Pennsylvania Avenue. Whatever the grand vision of Pierre Charles L'Enfant, architect of the capital city, had been, Angel thought sourly, it had certainly not been the gray and uninspiring view that stretched away toward Union Station from the rickety old building that housed the Department of Justice.

'However,' the Attorney-General said, reaching for a cigar, 'I'll give you a reason. You're still not fit.'

'I'm fine!' Angel expostulated, as the man behind the big desk lit the long black cigar and puffed huge clouds of smoke upward, patiently relishing the pungent odor. It smelled as if someone was burning a Sumo wrestler's loincloth, but Angel knew better than to voice his opinion of the Old Man's cigars. The Attorney-General thought that they were indubitably the best that money could buy – a little strong for some palates, perhaps – and did not know (or perhaps pretended not to know) that there was a mock reward poster stuck on a wall in the basement outside the Armory which offered a thousand dollars to the man who could find the Attorney-General's cigarmaker – and stop him from making any more.

'Of course,' the Attorney-General said. 'That's why you're using a stick.'

'Hell,' Angel argued. 'I'm using a stick because your damned quack downstairs insisted I use it.'

'Hmm,' said the older man, not really listening.

'Don't confuse me with the facts,' Angel said. 'I've already made up my mind.'

The Attorney-General looked up, as though Angel's sardonic remark had disturbed a train of thought. Then he nodded. 'Yes,' he said. 'Lorenz goes.'

Angel shrugged. He knew better than to argue. When the Old Man had made a decision, further discussion was academic. He couldn't argue with the Old Man's choice, either. Jaime Lorenz was a good man, one of the best in the department. He also had the advantage of being Spanish-American, which would be a useful plus in certain parts of Texas.

'When does he leave?' he asked.

'Tomorrow.'

'You mind if I take another look at that report?'

The Attorney-General pushed a slim

manila folder across his desk toward Angel. He smiled to himself as he did so. His top Special Investigator might be a fool for trouble, but he was without question the best man in the department. Even though he was still limping from the wound that the fugitive Magruder had put into his thigh a second before Angel had broken the arm holding the rifle, he was already itching to be back in the field. The Attorney-General knew that prolonged sojourns in the capital held few attractions for the tall man sitting opposite him. He had a fairly shrewd idea what those attractions were, as well, but he didn't air them. The relationship between his personal private secretary, Amabel Rowe, and his Chief Special Investigator was their own concern – mostly. His own damned trouble was that he liked having Angel around. It was good to talk over your problems with a man you knew you could utterly trust, a man who'd back you all the way down the line. There weren't many like that in Washington. Damned few anyplace else, come to that, he thought.

Frank Angel read once again the two-page handwritten report of Special Investigator Harker Nettery, who had heard something he felt worth transmitting to his chief in

Washington. It might be nothing: a rumor amplified in the telling along the owlhoot trail. On the other hand, it might be true, in which case the department should know and would act. The gist of the report was that there was a place on the Texas-Mexico border, somewhere around the Quemado area, where an endless supply of repeating rifles and other guns was available to bandits, Indian raiders, or *Comancheros* seeking to do business with both. The strange thing, Nettery said, was that no one would talk about exactly where it was, or who owned it. The Mexicans, he reported, crossed themselves when they spoke of the place, which they said was the home of the Devil himself. They called it *Valle del Muerto*, the Valley of Death. They said many of their people had died building it. Those who had survived would not speak of it. Rumor had it that anyone who started poking around asking about the place was liable to wind up dead, as was anyone who went searching for it or trying to penetrate the secrets of its owner. Nettery had come up with a name: the Valley of Death was owned by someone called Nix. Nettery added diffidently that he realized it was all hearsay and speculation, two commodities not in high regard at the department. He would have refrained from reporting had it not been for the case of a young Englishman named John Henry Tyrrell. Tyrrell had come to Texas from England, bringing enough money to buy land and stock for a ranch near the town of Madura. He was also planning to build a general store and open a bank there. He made a buying trip to St. Louis and while he was away, Comanches attacked his embryonic ranch, slaughtered his stock, and cut three of the men he'd hired to ribbons. A fourth survived long enough to tell Tyrrell that the Indians had been using Winchester repeaters of the very latest type, and Tyrrell got damned good and mad. He was neither blind nor a fool. Indians could only get that kind of firepower from white men, and Tyrrell swore that as God was his judge he would find the man who was supplying them. He had heard about Nix, and his storied valley, and he went out looking for both. He made no secret of his scorn for such childishness, or for those who feared it; when he left Madura – despite the advice of wiser heads who suggested caution, and the wisdom of waiting until the U.S. Marshal could be called into the case – everyone in the town knew that he was planning to find Nix, stick the barrel of a sixgun up Nix's nose, and tell him that if he didn't quit trading with the Comanch', he, John Henry Tyrrell, was going to spend every penny of his not-inconsiderable family fortune and every ounce of his undeniable energy to ensure that Nix went to prison for the rest of his damned, unnatural life.

Nobody ever saw him again.

The Tyrrell family in England, which was both rich and landed, chose not to accept the verdict of a dirty little town no more than a wide spot in the road that John Henry Tyrrell had bitten off considerably more than he could digest. They wrote to Her Majesty Queen Victoria's Foreign Secretary, the Right Honorable William Ewart Gladstone, requesting him to stir his Liverpudlian stumps. A request from such as the Tyrrells was as a command from elsewhere, and Gladstone took immediate action, writing to his friend the Secretary of State in Washington. State, knowing a hot potato when it saw one, had passed Gladstone's letter along to the Attorney-General like a shot. It married up neatly with Nettery's diffident information, and that was why Jaime Lorenz was packing his bags right now with a ticket in his pocket for the train up to New York, the steamer to Albany, and the Union Pacific to St. Louis. After a brief investigative halt there, he'd head on down to Texas.

'Funny name,' Angel mused. 'Nix.'

'Dime-novel stuff,' the Attorney-General snorted. 'Play-acting.'

'Nix.' Angel repeated, almost reflectively. 'Nothing.'

If it was perhaps the dime-novel stuff the Attorney-General said it was, it was damned effective for all that. It was the kind of name that would strike fear into the hearts of simple Mexican peasants, the kind of name that brutish frontier hardcases would remember. Yet it was too striking. Men took an alias to hide their identity, not to flaunt it. A man used another name to lose pursuers, or conceal their tracks, not so that those who heard it would never forget it. He laid down the dossier with a sigh, because it had all the hallmarks of a damned interesting case. He'd have liked to handle it himself, but the Old Man had already vetoed that.

'What have you got for me, Chief?' he asked.

'Ah,' the Attorney-General said. 'One of your old cases.'

'Which one?'

'Ernie Hecatt. Remember him?'
'He'd be hard to forget.'
'He escaped from Huntsville.'
'I know. About two and a half, three years ago. Disappeared.'
'That's it.'
'And?'
'There have been some sightings.'
'I know. I correlated them. Men who knew Hecatt. Said they'd seen him, called his name as he walked close by them, but he either didn't hear or ignored them. Walked on past as if he was deaf.'
'What do you think?'
'Mistaken identity, maybe.'
'Maybe,' the Attorney-General said. 'But you know my motto, Frank.'
Angel nodded. The Attorney-General committed his department to action on a very simple set of precepts. *Once,* he was fond of stating, *is mere happenstance. Twice, perhaps, is coincidence. But three times? Three times, gentlemen, means the bastards are doing it on purpose. And I want to know why!*
'How many sightings altogether?' he asked Angel now.
'Four. Five, if you count a "maybe",' was the reply. 'One in New Orleans. One in Jackson, Mississippi. One in Shreveport,

Louisiana, and another in St. Louis. The maybe was in Abilene. Abilene, Texas, not the Kansas one.'

'That's a pretty big area,' the Attorney-General observed.

'What I thought.'

'Check it anyway,' was the order, and Angel shrugged his agreement. The Old Man was handing him a nice easy number until he worked off the last lingering stiffness in his leg, giving him time to ease back into action rather than tossing him in, ready or not. It was damned thoughtful of the Attorney-General, but Angel wished to hell he wouldn't bother.

'Checking on Hecatt'll only take me a couple of days,' he offered. 'What do you want me to do then?'

The Attorney-General's smile showed he'd been hoping for Angel to say just what he'd said. 'Report to Kee Lai,' he said. 'For fitness tests.'

Angel gave a theatrical groan and got out of there.

THREE

The man known as Nix reined in the beautiful thoroughbred stallion and surveyed his kingdom. From Diablo Point, where he now stood, the tumbling land stretched away to the north, blurring to blue-gray on the horizons. It would not have mattered had it been pitch dark: Nix knew the country spread before him as he knew the contours of his own face, the shape of his own body. Better, perhaps, for he had created this place, which the Mexicans called *Valle del Muerto*.

It was well named.

To Nix's left, tumbling along the western edge of the land like gigantic rocks strewn carelessly by some Olympian god, lay the Burrow Mountains, thrusting their bare, jagged peaks eight, ten, sometimes twelve thousand feet into the empty sky. At their foothills lay the jagged black basalt of the lava beds, endless serried rank after endless wicked row. Neither man nor horse could negotiate them: they would cripple the larger animal in an hour, reduce the stoutest boots to ribbons in another, and the feet of a man to bloody ruin in half that time.

Below Diablo Point, which jutted out from the base of the mountains skirting the southern end of the valley, a long way below in the man-made clearing lay the *hacienda*. The land had been leveled, the L-shaped house built by thousands of sweating *peons* brought across the Rio Bravo for the paltry few dollars their labor commanded. They had been ferried back across the river when their work was done, unsure of where they had been, and warned never to speak of what they had created in the valley. One or two had: they had died ugly deaths that silenced all the others.

The house would not have shamed a wealthy landowner in Virginia, but there was a major difference: this was not only a house but a fortress, a castle. Around it stood a ten-foot-high stockade of pointed foot-thick logs, and at each side of the heavy wooden gates were high wooden guard platforms, duplicates of the ones at three of the four corners of the stockade. Guards manned the platforms at all times when Nix was there. Inside the stockade, a man-made miniature lake lapped at the edge of a stone patio which fronted the northern side of the house, sited for shade and coolness, refuge from the relentless sun. From the house a man-channeled river ran northward, falling gradually away with the natural slope of the valley, widening as it went. It had not been there when Nix came to this valley, any more than the virtually impassable barrier of chokethorn, briar, bramble, and creeper that lay like a mile-wide caterpillar across the northern edge of the valley. He had seeded the breaks and watered them, adding and adding and adding until the rioting bushes formed a tangled barrier through which even the hardy *javelinas*, the native wild pigs, could scarcely force a path. Nix said no man could get through the breaks, and no man had proved him wrong.

He turned now to the right, where broken cliffs backed by the plateaus that preceded the soaring San Miguel range lined the eastern skyline. Below them lay open prairie and scrubland – jackrabbit country, as one of his men had dubbed it – and to the north, desert as empty as the far side of the moon. Nothing good lived there: there was no water-hole, no life support of any kind. Only at its southern edge did the land miraculously bloom, between prairie and desert.

Almost in the dead center of the valley, between river and San Miguels, between desert and *hacienda*, a small wood stood. Beech, elm, some smaller deciduous trees and shrubbery clustered together, watered by a man-made tributary of the river which stemmed from the artesian well sited inside the stockade. Inside the little forest was a lake, around which Nix permitted the raiding Comanches who regularly visited his valley to camp. They came in through the narrow gap between the breaks and the San Miguels, empty desert that their own scouts constantly patrolled. No white man could have gone twenty yards in that country without being seen by the Indians. Nothing moves in the land of the Comanche that they do not see.

There was an entrance into the valley, of course.

Through the tangled barrier of the thorn-breaks ran a track. There were guardhouses at both ends of it, and a signal system between both that made it almost fool-proof. Even if some unwanted visitor were to overpower one set of guards – at either end – certain switches would infallibly be set, and the entire road be instantaneously turned into a murderous, booby-trapped defile of death.

South of the thornbreaks, between the woods and there, lay a huge, swampy lake. This was as far as the man-made river ran. There, the water became brackish, murky, smelling of old copper. Around it swamp plants flourished in the overheated dampness, and old trees drooped beneath the weight of hanging moss.

When there was quarry, many of them headed for the lake. There were other options, all of them clearly sign-posted. Nix smiled a cobra's smile at the thought: the Englishman, Tyrrell, had headed for the lake. He had almost made it, too. Almost was not good enough in Nix's valley. Those who lived in it, worked in it, those knew how to avoid its perils despite the absence of any semblance of a trail. Others ... others must fend for themselves. Nix's riders were strictly instructed and as strictly checked to ensure that when they traversed the valley, they left no tracks. A tumbleweed tied at the end of a length of rope affixed to the pommel would effectively blur the marks of a horse's hoofs. A spar of driftwood on an A-loop would flatten out tracks made during wet weather. The men used whatever would do the job, and always did it. They knew only too well what happened to anyone who challenged the will of their employer.

Nix sat now, solid and powerful in the beautifully tooled California saddle with its silver conchos and tapering *tapaderos*. The beautiful black stallion stirred as the wicked spade bit touched its sensitive jaw, shivering slightly, ready to move when commanded. Nix leaned forward and patted its sleek neck. 'Very soon, my beauty,' he murmured. 'Very soon now.'

He was a big man, wide of shoulder, solid and heavy. His hair and brows were as black as a raven's wing, and his deep-set eyes were dark, burning, almost fanatical. His physical presence made lesser men aware of their own comparative weakness. His chest was like a barrel, his thighs like hams. He stood well over six and a half feet without the soft, expensive boots, and weighed well over two hundred pounds, not an ounce of which was fat. There was only one imperfection in this enormous frame, and that was his left hand. Over it, Nix always wore a black glove which concealed an artificial hand. Specially made for him by the leading skilled men of Vienna, it was as close in appearance to a normal hand as anything made by man could be, but there was a difference. Some of his men had seen Nix use the hand as a weapon. It had become a steel claw, irresistible, terrible, and they feared it even more than the silver-plated Remington he wore and could use with such unnerving speed, or even the plaited rhinoceros-hide whip he carried looped to the pommel of his saddle.

His men feared Hercules Nix and he knew it, gloried in it.

He knew what fear was and he knew how to use it. He had spent nearly four long years amassing enough money to have power, and he had cheated and lied and finally killed to get it. Now that he had power, wealth, and strength, he used all of them ruthlessly, without pity. He gave no quarter, felt no doubt. He had learned that survival meant life and that life meant war and he intended to fight that war as he did everything else, relentlessly and totally. And as he did everything else, he would win. He would have his revenge, and go on from there.

'Thar he is,' Des Elliott said. He was a small, fair-haired, almost cherubic looking man dressed in a black leather jacket and pants against which his silver-studded gun-belt and nickel-plated Colts made an almost flashy contrast. He could have been anywhere between twenty and fifty, and he was the most sadistic and vicious of all Nix's hunting crew, the leader of his hired assassins.

'Where?' Nix said. His voice was throaty with anticipation. 'Where?'

'Way on up,' a second man said. 'Past the dry ford.'

The dry ford was the only safe way to cross the river. There were other fords, of course. Quarry found out the hard way which was which.

'He's done well,' Nix said, reluctantly.

'Yup,' the second man said. His name was Barnfield, but everyone called him Barney. He was long and lanky and he had a thatch of reddish-colored hair and three days of stubble on his chin. He scratched a match on the seat of his pants and set fire to a grubby-looking cigar butt.

'Looks like he's heading for the lake,' Elliott said, venomous satisfaction in his light voice. 'He ain't crossin'.'

'Good,' Nix said, his voice like iron now.

'Well, Boss,' a third man asked. 'How about it?'

'One moment more, Hisco,' Nix said. The skull-faced man who had spoken had the white hair and pink eyes of an albino. His mouth was like a razor-slash in the long jaw.

'Git ready, boys,' he murmured to those

behind him. He'd been on a hunting party before, and he knew what happened next. Even so, he was still startled when Nix gave a screech like a drunken Comanch' and drove the fine-tipped steel points of his Mexican spurs into the ribs of the beautiful black horse. The stallion contorted with pain and exploded into movement, going down the thirty-degree slope of Diablo Point as if it were a kitchen table, with Nix maniacally urging it to even greater speed. His cohorts did their nervous best to keep up with him but by the time they got to the bottom of the slope, Nix was already nearly half a mile ahead. Urging their animals to greater speed, they thundered in his wake, their dust rising behind them like a funeral pyre, a broad arrow of movement on the vast land whose point was Hercules Nix. The arrow was aimed unerringly at the tiny white figure moving slowly through the broken ground alongside the treacherous river.

Jaime Lorenz saw the dust and swore.

Men on horseback, that close, would be on him in less than half an hour. It didn't give him a hell of a lot of time to make it to the screening timber around the lake up ahead. Maybe he could make it, but it was going to be touch and go. He lurched on, trying to ignore the agony of his bloodily tattered feet. Every pounding footstep was like a bright lance of fire through his entire body, but he had to keep going or die, and he knew it. The sun had broiled his naked body, and his tongue was already thick with thirst. His lips were cracked, and he looked longingly at the purling river on his left. He shook his head doggedly. He wasn't about to risk that again. He kept on, his run hardly much better than a shambling walk, but moving on, a small defenseless speck in the hugeness of the land, ignoring the pleas of his overworked body for rest, water, and food. The timber up ahead was appreciably nearer when he looked up, and the sight gave him fresh strength. He caught the glint of water through the close-set trees, and dreamed for an instant of splashing in a deep, cool lake.

He risked a look over his shoulder. He saw the dust off to the rear, easier to see now, appreciably closer. He ignored the clear trail of blood spots he himself was leaving. They could see him, he knew. There would be no need of tracking until or if he got into the timber. He ignored everything now except the need to survive. Everything they had taught him in the training school, every technique, every trick was vital if he was to survive, get out of this deathtrap, and report what he had discovered here.

His brain checked, examined, and discarded idea after idea, trick after technique. He had to be realistic. He was naked, unarmed, and worn down by the exposure, minor wounds, and relentless pursuit. Until he reached the timber, he could not hope to make himself a weapon. He prayed to God he'd have the time. He could sure as hell use a break.

'There is no escape from my valley,' Nix had told him the night before. 'No escape at all. But you will try. You must. You know you must and I know you will. I will give you your chance. It is only a small one, but it is at least a chance.'

'Why are you doing this to me?' Lorenz had asked. 'Why is it necessary? If you want to kill me, why not just stand me up against a wall and shoot me?'

Nix had looked surprised and shocked. 'Do you think I am a barbarian?' he said.

'As a matter of fact,' Lorenz replied, 'yes.'

The words were hardly out of his mouth when Nix struck him down with the steel hand. It was a wicked punishing blow that numbed the entire side of Lorenz's body, and he lay on the ground retching in agony and looking up at the giant towering over him, madness glaring in his yellow eyes. It was then he had realized that Nix was going to do exactly as he had promised: turn him loose naked and unarmed in the hostile land, and then hunt him down like some animal. Quarry, Nix had said. You are merely quarry. And we kill it without remorse or pity.

They turned Jaime Lorenz out soon after sunrise. They told him he had a twenty-four hour start before they began the pursuit, but he did not believe that, although it was true. He moved away steadily eastward, away from the *hacienda*, heading for the long valley he had noted on his way into the area. It ran between the two lines of hills in the southeastern corner of the valley and Lorenz figured it might veer east even further, bring a man out above the Nucces country. He moved steadily, using the controlled jogtrot the Apaches used, the sun not unpleasant yet on his naked body. Later, he knew, he would have to find shade. He checked constantly for signs of pursuit, but there were none. Nor were there any trees or bushes big enough for him to fashion a weapon from. A bow and arrow, a spear, anything would be better than nothing. It would have to wait.

The long valley had turned out to be a blind canyon, with a sheer rock face at its southernmost end. There was a wooden sign set into the ground and Lorenz stood with his head down like a tired animal as he realized that this was all part of Nix's psychological warfare. The sign had a black skull and crossbones painted on it, and one word: WRONG! It was as if the big man was there in the canyon, jeering at him.

He knew that he had lost a lot of the advantage they'd given him. By the time he retraced his steps, sheltering from the fierce midday sun, it would be late afternoon. He shrugged fatalistically. When there was no choice, there was no choice. He had to work north after all, he had to do what he knew they would expect him to do: work north, toward the Portal, as they called the entrance road through which he had been brought in.

Morning found him halfway up the length of the valley. He had worked his way diagonally across the width of it, skirting the wooded glade without ever seeing any trace of the Comanche camp. At the edge of the river was a four-armed sign. Northward lay the lake, it said. Westward, lava beds. Northeast, desert, and back the way he'd just come: *Hacienda*.

Still no damned choice at all.

With a bob of the head for decision, he'd set off then toward the lake. He moved between stands of willow where they were available, even taking the risk of a kicking, cooling run through the shallowest edges of the river, relying on his speed to cancel out the danger of doing it. His breathing was more ragged now, though, and his heart thundered in his chest like a trapped beast. His whole chest felt as if it was on fire, and he wondered again whether that steel claw of Nix's had broken some of his ribs. There had been no time to fashion any form of defense, and now he knew that they were very close behind.

He plunged into the woods, heedless of briars and branches that whipped and tore his unprotected skin. Deeper and deeper into the screening trees he thrust, feeling the ground grow swampy, squishy, and wet and deliciously cool beneath his torn feet. Once he measured his length in the slopping mud, and its clammy embrace cooled, chilled his burned skin. Chattering birds fled ahead of him in panic, and he realized that he was making a lot of noise. Panic, he told himself. He thought of the dour instructor who'd taught him survival, imagined him standing watching with that disgusted expression he always wore when one of his charges blundered about like a panicked pig.

'That's it,' he would sneer. 'Nice and noisy, so they can find you with their eyes closed. Go on, make it easy for them!'

He stopped, poised like a hunted deer, letting his senses pick up the sounds of pursuit. They were close, but not closer. He tried to pinpoint them from the faint sound of their calls, but the dark dampness around him muffled sound. He moved forward again, but lifting his feet carefully now, setting them down warily, moving slowly and steadily through the darkening shadows where the swamp vegetation thickened. The earth gave off a damp, pungent, loamy smell and it was much cooler. He shivered slightly as he heard the eerie call of an unknown bird. Hanging moss brushed his naked skin like the finger of the dead.

'Jesus!'

Jaime Lorenz scrambled backward, flailing away and falling over as he clawed and bucked and wriggled to get away from the alligator on whose back he had just almost stepped. The beast turned idly in its muddy pit and regarded him with one awful, baleful eye. It yawned, showing a terrible set of razor-sharp teeth, and Lorenz shuddered. That mouth could take off a man's leg at the hip as clean as a wick-trimmer dousing a candle.

He moved away from the 'gator, shaking his head in numbed surprise. Who would have dreamed that madman had put alligators into the swamp? What other nightmares were there? Where there was one there were certain to be more, and it was no damned accident that they were here, any more than it was an accident that the fish in the river were the kind they were, or the jeering signs and the absence of waterholes were accidents. The whole valley was a carefully engineered death trap, designed to kill the unwary quarry as soon as it made its first mistake. If the human quarry avoided mistakes, it made no difference. Nix and his hunting crew killed it anyway. Which came first was only a question of how long it took.

He looked at his torn hands and nodded grimly.

He was damned if he was going to sit around and wait for Hercules Nix to come and get him. Given that decision, the next problem was what he could do to make it more difficult. He decided it was time to stop running and start fighting and the first thing he needed to do that was to make something to fight with. Hercules Nix and his killer crew might be going to kill him, but he was sure as hell going to hurt them while they were doing it. He looked at his hands again and saw that they were trembling slightly. Yes, he thought. The first one will probably have to be with the hands. After that – we'll see. He sat at the foot of the huge live oak and remembered his favorite line from Cervantes.

'Well, now,' he said to himself. 'There's a remedy for everything except death.'

Then he got up and went to meet the killers.

FOUR

One hundred days to the day of Jaime Lorenz's death in Nix's valley – although there was no way he could have known of the macabre anniversary – Frank Angel eased on foot through the high peaks of the empty mountains east of the Valley of Death. Autumn was already in the air, and there had been snow higher up, but at this level it was as hot as the hinges of the gateway to Hell. The sun beat down vertically on the faceless rocks of the high sierra, piling heat into them which they bounced right back into the face and body of the lone figure wending its way through the broken pass. Sweating under the heavy backpack and the exertion in this rarefied air, Angel moved doggedly on.

He had been trying to find a way through the mountains for four days now. There was always a way through, but first you had to find it. Sometimes you could spend more time backtracking out of blind canyons than you did moving forward, but sooner or later, inevitably, a determined man could and would find the defile that climbed up to the higher peaks and then slid alongside them and down to the other side. Angel was determined enough, and patient enough. Even though, in the thin mountain air, it was hard work just breathing, he kept plodding on, exploring, probing the mountain's defenses, retreating when his path was finally barred, thinking it through and then trying another way. He was going to find a way into the

Valley of Death, because whatever it contained had killed Jaime Lorenz, and Jaime Lorenz came from an elite corps of very hard-to-kill men. Which also meant that reconnaissance was necessary for survival as well as reckoning.

They knew Lorenz was dead after sixty days.

They didn't need any message, any notification, nor was there any. Indeed, it was the very absence of any word that confirmed the fact that Lorenz was dead. All of the department's investigators had two cutoffs, no more. No matter where you were, whatever you were engaged upon, you reported in as often as possible, but in none but the most extreme cases did you let the period between contacts exceed forty days. In extreme cases, you could extend it to sixty, but no longer. If you did not make contact in sixty days it was presumed – usually correctly – that you were dead. Whereupon appropriate steps would be taken in Washington.

The Attorney-General felt very strongly about having any of his men killed. Very strongly indeed. He took it as a personal affront to himself, as well as a slap in the face for the government he served. In fact, it was said that he felt so strongly about the killing of Lorenz that steam had been observed coming out of his nostrils. It wasn't true – not quite – but it made the point well. The Attorney-General made it plain that he wanted whoever had killed Lorenz, and he wanted him so badly that he could taste it in his whiskey. He had spent a very long time getting Presidential approval for his special force of thinking killing-machines, even longer finding the right men to train them. He was proud of his investigators: they were a product of a training course that weeded out any but the best, mentally and physically. The men who became Special Investigators for the Department of Justice were not only fully versed in the intricacies of federal and territorial law, but highly skilled practitioners of the martial arts. Physically tireless, matchless riders, superbly trained in the uses of all weapons, they were damned hard men to kill.

Which meant that Jaime Lorenz's killers were not to be taken on lightly. But taken on they most certainly were to be, and when the Attorney-General sent for Frank Angel, their conversation was not far short of perfunctory. Angel knew what the Old Man wanted, and the Attorney-General knew that Angel would do it. Or die trying to. They discussed what had to be discussed, and Angel rose to leave.

'Don't take any chances, Frank,' the Attorney-General had said as they shook hands. They always shook hands. Neither knew why, but they always did. Angel already had his grip outside the Attorney-General's office, a hack waiting at the door of the building. He would take the train up to New York, and catch a steamer from there to Galveston. As he told the Attorney-General, he wanted to come up on Nix gradual-like. Which was when the older man proffered his advice.

'You know me,' Angel grinned. 'When did I ever take unnecessary chances?'

'Get the hell out of here,' the Attorney-General grinned, 'before I have Amabel come in and make up a list!'

Amabel Rowe was the Attorney-General's personal private secretary, and if there had been any message in her usually merry blue eyes as she told him goodbye, Angel hadn't been able to read it. He wondered what she was doing right now, and then grinned at the thought that she was probably sitting in her office, in Washington, wondering what he was doing. He sent her a telepathic message across the miles between. What I'm doing is sweating, he told her.

Fall is a treacherous time in the Sierras. The nights can freeze you, while during the day the sun will fry off your skin. You have to wear clothes that will at least keep you warm at night, yet not leech the moisture out of you while you are on the move in daylight. Right now, Angel's woolen shirt and pants clung to him as if he had been hosed down, and the chill of the cool breeze, when it came around the shoulder of the mountain, was like a draft of clear cold water. He picked up his pace, for that slight movement of air could only mean one thing: he had found the way through the mountains. In a short while, he found himself on a rocky ledge looking down into a long valley already filling with the purple shadows of the afternoon. On its far side, the Burro Mountains tumbled along the horizon from the south on his left to the north on his right. Off on the edge of the northern fall of the valley he could see a line of trees, dark greens and browns contrasting with the dun flatness of the scrubland below. Shading his eyes with his hands, he thought he caught sight of a smoke smudge. He closed his eyes and opened them again, and this time he realized that what he could see was the *hacienda* that Davis had told him about. He could not make out any detail at this distance, but he didn't really need to. He knew the layout of the house, and to a lesser extent the valley, as though he had a map in front of him.

He'd found Davis in Galveston.

Welsh Al Davis, one-timer master builder, down and out and snoring like a pig in a Houston Street fleabag, just where they'd said he'd be. They'd also said that Al was a hopeless drunk, as dependent on the bottle as a babe on its mother's milk. The story – which Angel pieced together from two dozen men, a bit at a time – was that Welsh Al had gone down on the border someplace, building a *hacienda* for some got-rocks rancher. He'd come back with more money than Croesus, and with whatever he'd formerly been using for a backbone quite obviously removed. Welsh Al had a good reputation and a good business before he went down Mexico way, but he came back like a jigsaw with some of the pieces missing. His friends rallied around, tried to help out, but Al would have none of it. In short order he drank his way through his share of the business, his frame house on A Avenue in Galveston, his government bonds, his savings, and finally his loving and much put-upon wife. She ran off with a drummer when Al was so far over the hill that nothing could help him. Whatever it was he was trying to drown, folks said, there sure as hell didn't seem to be enough whiskey in Texas to do the job. Or maybe, as one wit drily remarked, the damned ghost could swim.

By the time Angel got to him, Welsh Al was seeing little green things on the walls, and he would have sold the veritable body of Christ for the price of a drink. Nevertheless, he was terrified of telling Angel the answers to his questions. He laid a trembling hand on Angel's forearm and begged him to keep secret the source of his information, begged him never to reveal how he had learned any of the secrets of Hercules Nix. Angel had gravely given his promise, knowing it wasn't worth a tinker's curse. As soon as Welsh Al got his belly full of tonsil-paint again, he himself would be telling anyone who'd listen. Angel was not inclined to believe that Hercules Nix had any spies in Galveston, although it mattered less than nothing if he had. He had never used his own name. All Nix would ever learn, if anyone asked, was that someone was poking about, someone talked to Welsh Al. There was no way for

Angel to know that within two hours of his leaving Galveston, Welsh Al was found in an alley off Skid Row with his throat cut, or that Hercules Nix knew full well who it was that was asking questions about his hidden valley.

So Angel stood now on the crest of the mountain and gazed with reflective eyes at Hercules Nix's kingdom. He knew all about the *hacienda* with its fort-like stockade, its interior defenses. He knew about the chromium steel bars on the windows, made of the same metal that James Eads had specified in the building of the bridge across the Mississippi at St. Louis. He knew about the two-inch-thick doors of solid oak lined with the same metal, and the reinforced concrete walls – faced with soft local stone to mask their harshness – built to the specifications of the German, Wayss. He knew the rough general topography of the valley in which the *hacienda* lay. He would have been appalled if he had known how little he actually knew but even so, it was a damned sight more than Jaime Lorenz had known. Had Lorenz found the place, or had they taken him and brought him in here? He might find that out soon.

The land below looked dry, burned,

barren. He could see no trails. He headed downhill, picking up speed as the heat went out of the sun and the slope ahead of him steepened. Another hour found him on the valley floor, moving northward along the wall of the San Miguels, heading for a long jutting spur of rock that pointed westward toward the sheltering trees he could see on the horizon. He planned to make a base among them, foraying outward to explore the valley, familiarize himself with Nix's domain. From a distance he looked like some small creature, antlike on the massive scale of the mesas.

In the lookout platform on the north-eastern corner of the stockade, Hercules Nix lowered the powerful telescope through which he had been watching Angel's progress.

'Looks like he's heading for the forest,' Elliott remarked.

'Yes,' Nix mused. 'Are any of The People there?'

'Mostly women an' kids,' Elliott replied. 'The men are off raidin'. As usual.'

'Good,' Nix smiled. 'We don't want anything – untoward – happening to our Angel. Not just yet, anyway.'

'How long you aimin' to let him run round

out thar, anyways?' Elliott asked. He was puzzled by Nix's curiously untypical reaction to the appearance of this intruder who had not only found a new way into the valley, but was being given its freedom. Normally, no matter where or how the perimeter had been breached, the appearance of any white or Mexican in the valley was the signal for Elliott and his men to be ordered out. They were not permitted to return to the stockade until the interloper had been run down and captured.

'As long as he wishes,' Nix purred.

'I don't get it.'

'The fact that you don't "get it", as you so elegantly put it, is a matter of supreme unimportance,' Nix told his lieutenant. 'The only important thing is that our little fly eventually finds his way into the spider's parlor.'

'You goin' to sit back, an' let him come on in here?'

'Of course.'

'You don't want us to go out an' get him?'

'No need. He'll walk right in.'

'How the hell can you be so sure of that?' Elliott wanted to know.

'Ah,' said Nix, with a smile like Death watching a knife fight. 'I happen to know the fly.'

And with that enigmatic explanation Elliott had to be content.

FIVE

It was a long time since Angel had lived off the land like an Indian, but it had been part of his training and it came back to him fast. Long ago, when they first brought him East to join the department, he had been taken first by train and then on horseback somewhere deep into a swampy wilderness far from any trace of civilization. They blindfolded him and plugged his ears before taking him out into the middle of the wilderness and turning him loose. He had no idea where he was. They gave him nothing, no food, water, or weapon. Somewhere in the wilderness, they said, was a 'safe' house. He had to find it. He had a one-hour start over the three men who would try to find and kill him. No other instructions, no other rules. Survive, they said.

He was out for four days.

When he finally found the 'safe' house, he

was eighteen pounds lighter, and as gaunt as a man who'd been a year in Andersonville. In the process of eluding his pursuers and coming safe home, he had learned many things. How to find water where none seemed to exist, or strain the worst filth out of brackish puddles through the cotton of his tattered shirt. How to trap, skin, and cook small wild things. Which berries were edible, and which would kill you (the birds taught you that). How to make a lair and conceal it as well if not better than any other hunted thing. All this he learned as he learned what they wanted him to know: how to survive. By the third day in the valley, had Nix sent his men out after Angel, he would have been hard to find and take. But Hercules Nix had no need to pursue Angel. He knew his quarry would come to him, and on the fourth night, Angel did.

He had learned a great deal about the valley by this time. Keeping to cover, moving little during the day, using twilight and night for exploration, the sleeping dawn for reconnaissance, he had spied unseen on the Comanche village upon which he had almost stumbled that first night. He assessed its probable strength by the number of teepees, women, and horses. Unseen in the night he watched the listless guards at the crude barrack half-hidden in the fringe of the thornbreaks at the northern end of the valley. He did not need to explore the breaks themselves, for Welsh Al had told him that they stretched over a mile, briars and thorn trees twining around the feet of logwoods and stunted oil palms and forming a barrier of formidable density. God alone knew what lived in there, Davis had shuddered, what reptiles and other horrors.

Angel had skirted the perimeter of the swampy lake, following its outline and testing its shore here and there. He had noted some of its denizens, moved to wonder why Hercules Nix had imported such exotic creatures, and to ponder over the madness that must thread through the man's brain. He had very soon learned to avoid the river and its savage population waiting for the unwary one who would use the dummy fords along its length. Only a sharp-eyed tracker, used to noting the minute marks that might enable him to follow where others could not, would have noticed that on the opposite bank of the river there were no tracks of any kind, no marks, no scarred rocks, nothing.

Now, wary of everything he could not see,

Angel made his way along the bank of the man-made river, using the advancing twilight to shield his movements from the guards on the stockade. By the time he had made his way to within striking distance of the *hacienda* the valley was as black as the inside of Satan's ovens. Through the tiny gaps between the logs of the fence Angel could see the lights of the house. Above him, the guards exchanged hoarse commonplaces. Just above the stockade on the northern perimeter a meshed gate such as is used in trout farms and fisheries was set between the river banks, and when he saw it Angel allowed himself a sour grin. Hercules Nix had peopled his wilderness with savage creatures, but he wanted none of them to infiltrate his personal domain. Inside the stockade, Angel knew, lay the man-made pool and the crucial well that supplied all the valley's water. He could hear the soft thump of its machinery as he eased around the edge of the stockade and wormed close to the western wall.

He had long since discarded his mountain clothing. Now he wore a black woolen shirt, black leather pants, soft black moccasins. He worked up a dirty daub with earth and spittle, striping his face with it so he would be harder to see. Then he checked his weapons and eased forward and down into the deep black shadows below the base of the stockade wall. The western side was by far the longest, its guard platforms further apart. From the map that Welsh Al had drawn, Angel had memorized the ground plan inside it. The *hacienda* was basically L-shaped, with the base of the L facing this long wall, shaded by English yew trees. He had long since decided that this wall afforded his best chance of getting inside the enclave unseen.

From beneath his woolen shirt he unwound the long silken rope that had been readied at his request by the Armorer in Washington. At one end was a flat unfolding metal bar that split into three to become a small grappling hook when he pushed onto the end of each bar three small rubber balls with barbed spikes. He swung the rope, lengthening it slightly on each swing, until he had enough play on it to loft it high into the night sky. Up, over, and down on the other side of the pointed stakes of the stockade it went, making a soft but audible bump as the spikes bit into the timber. Angel froze, waiting in the darkness like a trapped animal; but there was no challenge from the sentries. Nothing moved. He stood warily and tested the rope. It stretched slightly as he put all his weight on it, and then he went up the rough face of the stockade like a squirrel. Pausing at the top, he threw one arm over and checked for any sound of alarm. Hearing none, he unhooked the grapple and threw it down to the invisible ground inside the enclave. Below him was impenetrable darkness. He swung over the top of the fence and vaulted down. He rolled to break his fall, not silent but very quietly, and found himself among ornamental shrubs and bushes, perhaps fifty feet from the rear of the building. The soft thump of the pump was louder, more powerful. The ground trembled slightly with each stroke. Inside the house someone was playing the piano. Liszt, he thought, surprised.

Swiftly locating the rope and grapple, Angel disassembled it and stowed it in the many-pocketed pants. The rope he wound around his waist beneath the shirt. Then he squatted on the ground, taking the time to control his breathing, summoning the inner sense of presence that his Korean teacher, Kee Lai, had taught him long ago.

Then he moved like a prowling tiger toward the house.

Flattened against the wall, he eased along it until he came to the first of the tall, brilliantly lit windows. A rapid glance inside revealed a huge dining room, lit by cut-glass chandeliers, the table laid for dinner. The tablecloth was snow-white linen, the cutlery silver, the glasses sparkling crystal. Three place settings, he noted idly, wondering who Nix's guests might be. Then he worked around to the northern corner of the house, concealed by the blue-black shadows near the ground, until he could see the paved-stone patio in front of the pool. Over the patio was a loggia, from which depended grape-bearing vines and climbing plants whose flowers gave off a honeyed perfume. A low table and some chairs stood in the center of the sheltered patio, and a man came out of the house with a silver tray bearing a wine bottle and glasses which he proceeded to set out on the table. The man was short and squat and when he moved into the slab of light coming from the windows, Angel saw that he was an Oriental.

Now Angel eased around the front of the house, flat to the wall, moving like a stealthy predator, senses alert for the faintest sign of danger. The absence of guards was jarring, and he frowned. Inside the house, the Liszt sonata continued. Whoever was playing played beautifully, he thought.

Then all the lights went out.

'So, the sleeper awakes. Welcome, Angel. Welcome to the kingdom of Hercules Nix!'

Angel opened his eyes, and the blurred figure standing above him became clear as focus returned.

'You?' he said. He tried to get up, then winced as he felt the stiffness of the muscles in his neck.

'Me,' Nix said. 'I am surprised you remember me so well.'

'I remember you. Hecatt,' Angel said, sitting up and looking around. He was in a sumptuously appointed bedroom with velvet drapes on the windows and what looked like an Aubusson carpet on the floor. 'You're the kind nobody ever forgets.'

'I am pleased to hear it,' Nix replied. 'More than you can imagine.'

'You're Hercules Nix?'

'That is correct. The man you once knew as Ernie Hecatt is, to all intents and purposes, dead and buried. In his place stands one of the richest men in the United States – I, Hercules Nix!'

'You can call a rat any damned thing you

want,' Angel said flatly. 'It's still a rat.'

His host's darkly smiling mien changed suddenly to a black mask of anger, and the gloved left hand drew back as if to strike Angel down. Then, with a huge indrawn breath, Nix controlled his anger and pasted the smile back on his face. Only the eyes, burning like fire, betrayed the passion beneath the surface. 'Oh, no,' he said, softly. 'You'll not enrage me, Angel. I have waited far too long to spoil my pleasure. There will be no cheap escape for you.'

'Escape? What are you talking about?'

'Surely you do not think you are here by accident?'

'I'm not?'

'My dear Angel, I thought you would be flattered at all the trouble I have taken to get you here.'

'I'm flattered, I'm flattered. Now tell me what the hell you're talking about.' Angel said. He swung his legs down to the floor and got to his feet warily. His head swam slightly, but that was all. 'How did I get up here?'

'Yat Sen,' Nix said. 'My valet. I found him in San Francisco, where he was working in a hand laundry. He has passed through every known level of the martial arts, Angel. I have heard that the Justice Department teaches these skills.'

'Have you, now?' Angel parried.

'Let me warn you just once,' Nix said silkily, 'not to be foolhardy. Yat Sen would be to your puny abilities what a Grand Master would be to a beginner at chess.'

'Sure,' Angel said, letting his scorn show.

'Just remember that he came across twenty feet of open ground to stun you and you did not hear as much as the whisper of his feet.'

'True enough,' Angel admitted, remembering. He had never heard of any man possessing the skills that Nix boasted his man had. That didn't mean it wasn't possible. He decided to repeat an earlier question.

'My dear Angel, I have been expecting you confidently ever since I first started trading with The People – the Comanches, in this case. Isn't it amazing how all these Mongolian savages refer to themselves as The People? To tell you the truth, I was a little disappointed that it took so long to attract you to my little, ah, hide-away. I thought at first that the Tyrell business would do it, but instead you sent someone else.'

'Jaime Lorenz,' Angel said.

'He was very clumsy, Angel. Clumsier

even than you, and you were very obvious. My men took him outside San Antonio and brought him here.'

'He's dead, then?'

'Alas, yes. So very few men survive the, ah, rigors of the valley. But he served his purpose. I knew that when he arrived, your coming was but a matter of time. What is it, sixty days after departure you assume death?'

'You know a lot about the department.'

'Lorenz told me a lot.'

'So you knew I was coming?'

'Of course. Your movements from the moment you arrived in Galveston have been reported to me. You have been under observation every inch of the way.'

'You seem to have it all buttoned up,' Angel said.

'Ah, do not think you have an ace up your sleeve, my dear fellow. I'm afraid your arrival through the mountains was also observed. I've been watching your every move.' He smiled at the look of chagrin on his prisoner's face, and bowed sardonically.

'Why did you let me stay out so long? Why didn't you send your boys out to get me?' Angel asked.

'What, and spoil my pleasure?' Nix said, throwing back his huge head and laughing.

'After I have gone to so much trouble to arrange everything? No, no, my dear Angel. I wanted you to have every advantage. I wanted you to know just exactly what you were up against here in my valley. And I am sure, now, that you do know. So you, as well as I, may relish what comes next.'

'Which is?'

'Oh, come, not now,' Nix smiled. 'This evening you will dine with me. I want to spend some time with you. It may surprise you, Angel, but I respect your abilities. I confess myself eager to discover just how good you are. But that is tomorrow. Tonight ... well, perhaps you are like Scheherazade. Perhaps for you there will be no tomorrow.'

'You'll have to excuse me,' Angel said harshly. 'I'm not really kitted out for a dinner party.' He gestured at his mud-smeared face and hands, his soiled clothing, comparing it with the fine black broadcloth suit of his captor.

'I'm afraid I won't take no for an answer,' Nix said, showing his teeth. 'We have plenty of time to take care of your needs.' He clapped his hands once, and then again. As if by magic the Oriental, Yat Sen, appeared in the doorway. He bowed without speaking.

'Mr Angel's bath is ready?' Nix asked

expansively. Yat Sen bowed again, yes.

'Good. Look after him, Yat Sen. We dine at nine, Angel.'

He went out through the tall double doors, and the Oriental looked at Angel expectantly.

'Please no trouble,' he said quietly. Like many of his race, he had difficulty with the pronunciation of the r's and l's. 'Trouble' came out 'tlubber.' Angel nodded as Yat Sen stepped to one side, and gestured, this way. He reckoned correctly that it would take five steps to be beside the Oriental, and on the fifth step he was moving very fast, his hands perfectly right, his body beautifully set for the blow which he delivered sideways at Yat Sen's carotid artery. Nine hundred and ninety-nine men out of a thousand, tenfold, would have been killed on the spot by the blurring hand. Not one in a million could have done what Yat Sen then almost casually did. He intercepted Angel's hand. All Angel's strength, all his speed, and all his skill were behind the blow, yet the Oriental caught it in midair the way a kid catches a bouncing ball, and he held it totally immobile with the most astonishing strength Angel had ever encountered.

'Please,' Yat Sen said. 'Take bath, no tlubber.'

Angel looked at his own hand held fast in the unbudging fist of the Oriental, and he let out his breath in one long, astonished sigh. 'Yat Sen,' he said. 'That was impossible.'

'Not impossibar,' Yat Sen said, handing him a fragrant bar of toilet soap. 'Enjoy bath. I get crothes.'

Angel shook his head silently as the Oriental padded out of the bathroom. Then he quickly got out of his dirty clothes and slid into the soft water. He was direly in need of a bath, and soaped himself vigorously, getting rid of the accumulated dirt of his outdoor days. As he bathed, he let his mind range over the things he had learned in the last few hours. The supreme, almost contemptuous, confidence of the man who called himself Hercules Nix, formerly Ernie Hecatt, trickster, thief, and murderer. He was still all these things: he had virtually admitted responsibility for the death of Tyrrell, and had undubitably had Jaime Lorenz killed. This astonishing house, the awesome, casual power of the Oriental, Yat Sen. The killing country that lay beyond the safety of the stockade, with the Comanche camp at its heart. A battalion of cavalry would have its work cut out making a successful attack on

Nix's stronghold. One man, even if he were free, would seem to have no damned chance at all. He cursed himself for allowing Nix to take him with such contemptuous ease, like a man catching goldfish in his own pond. He looked up as Yat Sen came back into the steamy bathroom.

'Crothes leady,' Yat Sen said. 'Want shave?'

'Leave the razor on the shelf,' Angel said casually. 'I'll do it myself.'

Yat Sen's face changed slightly, and Angel realized that he was witnessing the nearest expression Yat Sen had to a smile.

'Ah, solly,' the Oriental said. 'Might cut Yat Sen thloat instead.'

'Yat Sen!' Angel said reproachfully. 'Would I do a thing like that?'

'Bet you ass,' Yat Sen said. 'Get out bath. I shave.'

'OK,' Angel grinned. 'But you turn your back, now.'

Yat Sen's face contorted again in its strange impersonation of a smile. 'You damn blave,' he said. 'Or damn stupid. Not know which.'

'Flattery will get you nowhere,' Angel said.

Half an hour later, immaculate in a dark blue three-piece suit with wide lapels cut in the latest style, and a fine cambric shirt with diamond studs and buttons which fitted him quite well, Angel descended the ornate staircase and followed Yat Sen into the drawing room. It was beautifully furnished to disguise its main fault, a low, beamed ceiling, and managed even so to appear light and spacious. The furniture was very old and obviously very expensive. Angel knew very little about antiques, but he knew when he was looking at them. There were not many pieces in the room less than a hundred and fifty years old.

Hercules Nix came beaming to meet him, as if Angel were an old and honored friend arriving in his own coach at some Georgetown dinner. Nix handed him a glass of Amontillado and as he did, the gentle music from the ornate rosewood piano in the far corner of the room stopped. One of the most beautiful women Frank Angel had ever seen stood up behind it and smiled at him.

'My dear,' Nix said, smiling at Angel's expression, savoring the moment. 'Come and meet our guest, Mister Frank Angel, who works for the Department of Justice in Washington. Angel, this is my wife Victoria.'

SIX

'Well,' Victoria Nix said, rising from her seat at the table. 'If you will excuse me, gentlemen?'

She smiled at Angel, who smiled back as he and her husband rose and stood silently as she went out of the dining room, the silk of her gown rustling, the piled-high auburn hair catching bright highlights from the shining chandeliers. She had hardly spoken during the meal, and it had become immediately apparent to Angel that whatever her relationship to Hercules Nix was based upon, it was not love. She had flinched visibly every time he turned toward her, the way an often-beaten dog will. Unless spoken to directly, she had kept her eyes cast down, a dreamy expression behind them.

Angel turned to see Nix watching him. 'She's very beautiful,' he said.

'Of course,' Nix said, offhandedly, the way a man will acknowledge a compliment about the horse he is riding.

'Where did you meet?'

'We first met, ah, near her home. Her father owned a ranch on the Brazos above Waco.'

'How long was it after your escape?'

'Quite soon, as a matter of fact,' Nix said urbanely. He selected a cigar from the humidor that Yat Sen had brought into the room on noiseless feet. He rolled it between his fingers, listening to the crackle of the leaves. He sniffed it, and then nodded, giving it back to Yat Sen, who trimmed it with a gold cigar-cutter and then came around the table to perform the same service for Angel. The cigars were fine Havanas, and the smoke curled lazily toward the brilliant lights in the still air.

'So that's where you went to ground,' Angel mused aloud. Nix smiled.

'You're perspicacious, Angel. I'll tell you the rest to save you guessing. Old Tom Stacey – Victoria's father – was not only the man who saved my life. He was the very foundation of my fortune.'

'You had nothing,' Angel pointed out. 'How come?'

'Good management. Good fortune. And a little manipulation.'

'You stole it.'

'Oh, come, let's not be crude, my dear

fellow. I prefer to think of it as long-term forward credit.' Nix smiled like a man pleased with a turn of phrase.

'Like I said,' Angel repeated. 'You stole it. What did you do, sell dud bonds?'

'You're quite close to the truth, actually,' Nix admitted, leaning back in his chair and stretching expansively. 'But it wasn't quite so blatant. I really am not the blatant type, you know.'

'You know what I said about rats,' Angel reminded him, and was rewarded by a quick flare of anger in the yellow eyes. But it lasted only a moment, and Nix smiled his self-satisfied smile again.

'My dear Angel, I know you are not a stupid man. You will oblige me by not pretending to be obtuse. Do you wish to hear the story or not?'

'Go ahead. I've got noplace to go at the moment.'

'I like that "at the moment",' Nix purred, 'but let it pass. So: the story. Actually, it was almost childishly easy. I went to live with the Staceys when I was well again.'

'Well? You were sick?'

'I was sick, all right,' Nix snarled. 'I had to cross half of Texas on the dodge, Angel! I had to fight off a bunch of Comanches who put a hole in my arm that caused this–' He raised his iron hand and slammed it down on the table, making the coffee cups jangle. 'I was three-quarters dead of hunger and thirst and loss of blood. If it hadn't been for Victoria finding me, getting help, I'd be dead now.'

'No way she could have known that,' Angel said, sardonically. 'I won't hold it against her.'

'Ah, yes,' Nix said, relaxing, smiling like a skull. 'I remember you had a penchant for mordant humor. That's as well, for you'll be in need of it ere long.'

'You were saying how sick you were,' Angel said, impatiently.

'Yes,' Nix hissed. 'I was ill. But I pulled through. Do you know how I pulled through?'

'Because you're such a wonderful human being?'

'Because I wanted revenge, Angel!' Nix said, ignoring the other man's shaft. 'I wanted revenge! I swore as I lay dying that I would survive, that I would pull through. I wanted to live so that one day I would be able to kill you!'

'Join the club,' Angel said. 'There's a lot of members.'

'I don't doubt that,' Nix said, drawing in a deep breath. The angry light in his eyes faded again, and Angel again noted the big man's iron control. 'At any rate, I discovered that Tom Stacey was a poor enough rancher and an even worse businessman. He was one of the directors of a cattleman's bank in Waco, and it was going to the dogs. I soon showed him where he was going wrong, and how to put it right. He was – grateful.'

Angel nodded. Nix had obviously chosen to forget that as Ernie Hecatt he had been a liar and a cheat and a thief. He was proud of having helped to set the little cattleman's bank on its feet – no doubt so that he could rob it the better. Not for the first time, Angel marveled at the capacity of the human race to delude itself. But there was no point in saying this to Nix. Angel leaned back and listened.

'Pretty soon, old Stacey asked me to look after his interest in the bank. Then they made me manager. Soon after that, I discovered that among the assets were half a million dollars' worth of twenty-five-year government bonds. They were just sitting in the safe, waiting for the 1890s to roll around when they'd mature. Ready money. Nobody would dream of checking on them for years.

It was a perfect opportunity and I took it. I sold them, taking a thirty percent discount on face value, and used the money to buy guns in St. Louis. Then I did some trading with the *Comancheros*. Within a year I had multiplied my original stake tenfold.'

'So you put the money back, of course.'

'Of course – not! I realized there was a fortune waiting to be made, and I went out and made it. I made direct contact with the customer, cut out the middle-man. I used my money to make the necessary contacts, entertained royally. And all the while, I was making plans to build this place.'

'Those deals you made,' Angel interposed. 'Where did you go to make them?'

'I'm not sure, I recall several in New Orleans. A couple of times in Shreveport. Why do you ask?'

'Abilene, Texas?'

'It could be. Why?'

'Indulge me,' Angel said. 'I'm just curious.'

Nix shrugged, and Angel grinned to himself. At least he had support for those sightings that had been reported to the department, which could be useful when he got back to Washington. If he ever did. He was some way from doing it right at the moment. He tuned in again to Nix's monologue.

'...told Stacey I was thinking of setting up on my own, and wanted to look around for a ranch. The old fool was pleased. I told him I wanted to marry his daughter. He wasn't too keen on that, but I managed to persuade him. I pointed out the fact of the missing bonds, and that all the transactions had been countersigned by him as a director of the bank. I said I'd blow the whistle on him if he didn't do what I wanted. He was no trouble after that.'

'And his daughter?'

'I wanted her,' Nix said, without expression. 'And so I took her.'

There was a long, empty moment of silence. Nix puffed expansively on his cigar and then waved a regal arm.

'And this is what I built. The Valley of Death, as they call it.

'Impressive,' Angel said.

'Indeed it is,' his host smiled. 'I wonder if you realize just how impressive?'

'Tell me,' Angel suggested.

'I'll tell you,' Nix smiled, his expression as cold as the belly of a water-moccasin. 'I'll tell you, for instance, that even if, in the farthest reaches of your imagination, you were to think you might escape the stockade, you would be blown to smithereens before you had covered thirty feet outside.'

'How come?'

'Simple enough. The perimeter outside the stockade is mined.'

'But–'

'You were going to point out that you walked through that perimeter and were not blown up?' Nix chided. 'Come, Angel. Use your intelligence.'

'You knew I was coming, and so–'

'I switched off the circuit.'

'You switched ... you just lost me again.'

'I will explain,' Nix said patiently. 'The mines are buried explosive devices. Each is linked to the other by a series of copper-sheathed wires. Those wires can carry an electrical current, which can be switched on or off.'

'Electricity? But how can you produce electricity out here?'

'Batteries, Angel, batteries. Must I explain it in words of one syllable? I was led to believe you were an educated man, not a dolt. Electricity is not viable on any scale, everyone knows that. No means has yet been found to produce it. Nevertheless, I have followed carefully the experiments conducted by Gaston Plante in 1859 by which a means was manufactured to produce electrical current. It is called a lead-acid battery. Clumsy, and very expensive, but it works. I have the materials to make these batteries here, and they provide power which can be switched on or off at will. For special occasions, of course: I do not keep them on all the time. It is hardly necessary, anyway.'

'Don't they discharge anyway, whether you use them or not?'

'Over a period of time they do go flat, true. It is a laborious and expensive business to replace the plates, but I have money, and I use it to buy what I want. Whatever that may be.'

There was a momentary silence before the big man spoke again.

'Have you ever been in prison, Angel?' he asked.

'Once,' Angel replied. 'But not for long.'

'Then you have no real conception of the reality,' Nix said. 'No idea of what it's like. Have you?'

'No.'

'They degrade you, Angel. They depersonalize you. They make you a number, and then they throw you into the filth, the stink, to live and sleep and eat with animals! Animals! Nobody gives a damn whether you live or die. The guards bully and beat you, try to reduce you to a groveling beast. It is hell, Angel. Unadulterated hell. It cannot produce anything except a thirst for vengeance, retribution!'

'Tell that to the people you robbed,' Angel said. 'See how they feel about it.'

'Pah!' Nix snorted. 'If God hadn't wanted them to be sheared, he wouldn't have made them sheep!'

'Twelve of those sheep finally put you into Huntsville, Nix,' Angel said. 'Never underestimate them!'

'No!' Nix hissed. 'You put me there, Angel. You! Because of you, I spent a year in that hell on earth. And do you know, there wasn't a day that I didn't think of you, curse your name, vow to kill you because of what you'd done.'

'Very dramatic,' Angel said flatly. 'And not a bit convincing. You're just trying to justify yourself, Nix!'

Again, Hercules Nix released his breath in a long sigh, controlling his burning anger. 'You may be partly right at that,' he admitted. 'Nevertheless, I have prepared for my revenge on you, and tomorrow, I will have it. Tomorrow, at dawn.'

'Dawn?' Angel said. 'Listen, if I oversleep, you just start right in without me.'

Nix smiled. 'I admire bravery,' he said, 'but you are merely cocky. That will not help you much when you are alone in the valley, naked and unarmed.'

'Naked and unarmed, is it?' Angel said. 'I didn't know about that. But it figured you wouldn't give a man half a chance if you could avoid doing it.'

'You will have your half-chance, Angel. It will be twenty-four hours before we come after you. In that time you can prepare yourself any way you wish, go in any direction, hide, run, stand and give battle. Anything you like. Your man Lorenz had no weapons, but he killed four men before he was taken.'

'Good,' Angel said. 'Pity he didn't get you, Hecatt.'

His captor smiled an Olympian smile. 'Understand, Angel, I will not be angered, even by your using my – other name. Tomorrow, you will provide a long-awaited diversion, but that is all. You are not important in the ultimate scheme of things. This valley is the important thing. It is already fast becoming the biggest center in the area west of the Mississippi for the sale of arms, and it will become bigger, bigger.

With that growth will come power. They will all come to me – Comanche, Apache, Kiowa, Lipan, all of them. And the others, the renegades and the revolutionaries from below the border!'

'You don't care that the guns you sell kill innocent women and children? You don't lose any sleep thinking of that?'

Nix laughed aloud, a short, sharp bark of sound. 'Are you mad?' he snapped. 'I care for nobody, nobody but myself. I learned that in the sink of hell you sent me to, Angel. I learned that only the strong survive, only the rich have power, only the strong and powerful can do as they please. As I can, now. In a few years I will own part of Texas. A few more and Senators, Congressmen will seek my advice, do my bidding as they used to! I will rule this land!'

There was a fanatic glow in the deepset eyes, and Angel knew that in thought if not in person, his captor was some other place, not here in the room with him. He sought to pop the bubble of Nix's vainglory.

'You're forgetting something,' he said harshly.

'What? What's that?'

'The Department of Justice,' Angel said. 'They know where I am. They know about you. If I go missing, there'll be another man, and another, and another, and in the end they'll get you and hang you!'

'If it pleases you to try to bluff me, Angel, go ahead,' Nix smiled. 'However, I happen to know that you made no report to Washington. They do not know where you are. And even if they did, what could they do? Let them send another man. Let them send fifty, a hundred, and they will never enter my valley unless I wish it. My ally Koh-eet-senko will see to that!'

'Koh-eet-senko? Is that the Comanche leader?'

'Correct. I notice that you do not make the common error of using the word "chief" as so many people do.'

'I know something about Indians,' Angel said. 'I know something about your friend Koh-eet-senko, too. He's a bloodthirsty butcher, him and all his tribe. What do they call themselves–?'

'The Timber People,' Nix said. 'You are right. It is they your Department of Justice would face if they attempted to try to take me here. I'd be extremely surprised if any of them survived to repeat the experiment. My allies are, as you know, extremely well-armed.'

'I know it,' Angel said. 'How come you're so friendly with them?'

'It was not a problem,' Nix said. 'I took the trouble to study their history, their culture, their background. Koh-eet-senko was extremely impressed to meet a white man who could talk with him on almost equal terms about the history of his people.'

'I imagine he was more impressed to meet a white man who would sell them repeating rifles,' Angel said drily.

'There was that,' Nix smiled. 'But my study of these savages was psychological as well as historical. I was able to predict their reactions to certain sets of circumstances. They are basically very simple, very childlike.'

'Sure,' Angel said. 'Tell it to Matilda Lockhart.'

'Who?'

'Matilda Lockhart. Comanches carried her off in 1838. They took her to their camp and gave her to the men. All the men in the tribe, Nix. When the men were through with her, the women got started. They burned her all over her body with blazing sticks, burned her nose right off her face. They made her a slave. They punched her and kicked her black and blue if she so much as whimpered. She was exactly sixteen years of age.'

'Pah!' Nix said, scornfully. 'You can't influence my thinking with these horror stories, Angel. The Comanches believe women are just chattel. They treat them accordingly. Anyway, I expect that story was wildly exaggerated. You know how these frontier crones gussy up atrocity stories. That's how they get their jollies.'

'You really don't give a damn, do you?' Angel said.

'No, I don't. I told you already, Angel. I only care about myself. Nothing else matters. I live for the moment from day to day. Right now, you are the top priority in my life. Tomorrow, or whenever we finish our little – game – something else will take your place.'

'Like your barbarian friends and the guns you sell them.'

'My barbarian friends, as you call them, have a long and fascinating history. Do you know anything about them?'

'Yes,' Angel said. 'I do.'

'Then tell me how they got their name.'

'It was misspelled by some Spaniard who was the first to see any of them. The Comanch' are really Rocky Mountain Shoshone.

They were known to the Utes as *Koh-mats*, meaning "those who are against us", or "enemies". It was the Ute word that the Spaniards misspelled as *Komantciá*, and which the whites bastardized to Comanche. They are really descendants of the *Nermernuh*, the Shoshone.'

'I see you do know about them,' Nix said. 'You are an unusual man, Angel.'

'I'll bet you tell all the boys that,' Angel said. 'You're a phony, Nix!'

'Phony, my dear fellow? What can you possibly mean?'

'All this claptrap about having studied the Comanch', the honorable past. You're justifying yourself selling them guns that they kill white settlers with. You may be rich, but it's blood money you're rich on.'

'It spends the same as the other kind,' Nix said, getting up out of his chair. 'Come, we are keeping the lady waiting.'

Angel followed him out to the patio. It was cool now, and Victoria Nix wore a lacy, woolen shawl around her formerly bare shoulders.

'You'll take coffee, Mister Angel?' she asked. Her voice had the soft lilt of the South in it, and Angel nodded, smiling. Victoria Nix was slim and quite tall. Her bare arms were slender and faintly golden from the sun. The rich glow of her auburn hair made her wide green eyes seem darker, more somber. Once again, Angel was struck by her sheer beauty, and the bizarreness of her marriage to Hercules Nix. He watched as she nervously checked to see if her husband approved of her speaking, the way her eyes dropped when he smiled blandly at her.

'You'll have a brandy, Angel?' Nix asked.

'I believe I will,' Angel said, and when Nix handed him a brandy glass with a generous measure of the golden liquid in it, he discovered that it was French brandy, and very old. 'You do yourself proud,' he remarked. 'Isn't it hard to freight all these things in?'

'Not hard,' Nix said. 'Expensive, certainly. But only that. If you are prepared to pay for it, everything is obtainable. Without exception.'

Angel wondered whether he had imagined Victoria Nix's shudder as her husband spoke these words. He certainly did not imagine the way she smiled at him automatically, anxiously, as he put his arm around her shoulders and hugged her once, in a proprietary fashion, or the way she immediately disengaged herself from his grasp. She sat in a chair immediately opposite Angel and stared into her coffee cup. After an awkward silence, she looked up.

'Will ... will you be staying long, Mister Angel?' she asked.

Nix intervened before Angel could open his mouth. 'Our guest can only stay the one night, my dear,' he said. 'He has to leave at daybreak.'

'If I'd known the company would be this pleasant, I'd have planned a longer stay,' Angel said. 'But I'm afraid I, ah, have no choice.'

It seemed to him that she understood what he was saying, although he had been convinced she had no idea of her husband's plans for him on the morrow. Just what was causing the deep, swimming anxiety in her lovely eyes he could not fathom. Whatever it was, it demonstrated that there was something very, very wrong in the relationship between Hercules Nix and his wife. She was in mortal fear of his very touch.

Now Nix put down his coffee cup with a decisive movement, and rose to his feet, stretching his arms wide and yawning ostentatiously. As if on signal, Victoria Nix got up, putting down her coffee unfinished. Angel stood up, but Nix waved him back to his chair.

'No, no, my dear fellow,' he said. 'Finish your coffee. Victoria and I always turn in early. You stay here, enjoy the evening. Yat Sen will bring you another brandy.' He offered his arm to his wife, who took it gingerly. 'I'll see you in the morning.' Nix said, and smiled like a cobra.

They walked toward the door, and as they reached it, Angel heard Victoria Nix exclaim impatiently. A moment-later, she came hurrying back.

'My wrap,' she said loudly. 'I left it on the chair! Goodnight again, Mister Angel!'

He was about to echo her words when she lowered her voice and bent close to him. She smelled of some fragrant perfume.

'For God's sake!' she hissed in an agonized whisper. 'For God's sake, Mister Angel – get me out of this place!'

SEVEN

They turned him loose at dawn.

It was a strange, almost ghostly scene. Hercules Nix stood like some graven idol, his men bayed behind him in a half-circle, watching with almost sardonic amusement as one of them ripped off Angel's clothes. When they were done, he nodded.

'You have a whole day, Angel,' he said. 'Don't waste it.'

No trace of his urbanity of the previous night remained. He was cold and remorseless, and Angel clamped his teeth together so that the chill of the dawn wouldn't make him shiver. The huge wooden gates were thrown back. On the gullied sides of the burros, light touched the rocks enough to make some of the darker shadows contrast with others.

'Git movin', Angel,' Des Elliott said with a leering grin. 'Flap your wings!'

Angel shook his head ruefully, and spat into the dirt at Nix's feet.

'You're as crazy as a bug in a box,' he said flatly. Without waiting to see Nix's reaction, he turned and loped away from the stockade, his mind already intent on survival. He had no illusions about dying bravely, with a quip on his lips as they did in those stiff-upperlip stories for British boys. If there was any dying to do, he sure as hell didn't intend it to be him who did it. He headed north along the edge of the river. After a while he looked back, but they were already gone, the gates of the stockade shut. He moved on, steadily. The gray land beneath the pinking dawn sky was as empty as the land of Nod before God sent Cain there.

After a while, Angel veered eastward, keeping up a steady jogtrot that he varied every fifteen minutes or so by walking for the same length of time. He had spent much of the night working out his movements, and until he reached his first destination, he could let his mind rove over the things he had learned during his stay in the Nix *hacienda*.

The most stunning, the most unexpected surprise had been the agonized appeal for help from Victoria Nix. What was behind it, Angel could only guess, but it reinforced his impression that there was something hugely wrong with the relationship between the woman and her husband. There had been no sign of her when Yat Sen had brought him down to the big living room in the pre-dawn darkness. He imagined she was kept away from the less savory of Nix's activities on purpose. She had certainly given no indication that she knew what her husband planned for their guest. Either way, there had been nothing he could do. He could not even get a message to her, and did not see her again. Her terror-drowned eyes stayed in his mind all through the night. Now as he jogged across country he saw them again, and shook his head. His first priority was his own survival. From what he had been told by Nix, he would need all his craft and cunning.

'Tyrrell, Tyrrell?' Nix had said. 'Oh, the Englishman. Yes, he came up here. Angry as hell. Claimed I'd sold guns to the Comanches and they'd killed some of his people. I said there was absolutely no proof that what he said was true. He damned my eyes and said he aimed to get some proof and stick it up my nose!'

'What happened then?' Angel asked, feeling quite certain that Nix was lying, lying because it was a more interesting way of telling the story rather than for any gain. From other hints in the man's conversation,

Angel was fairly sure Tyrrell had been given the same treatment that was awaiting him. But Nix went on with his embroidered yarn.

'He said he was damned if he wasn't going to ride over to the Comanche camp and talk to Koh-eet-senko himself. I warned him of the folly of such an action, but he was beyond listening to advice. He went out of here like a bat out of hell, and I never saw him again.'

'You knew he was dead, though.'

'Of course. There is little that happens hereabouts I don't know of. But I could scarcely be held responsible for what Comanches do to a white man they find skulking about on their land.'

'Land you provide for them.'

'I believe in coexistence, Angel. It suits my convenience, and it is infinitely less wearying than constant war, as well as infinitely less dangerous. I observe their rules; they leave me alone. It is not the best of worlds, but it's better than living in constant fear.'

'But you do. You're guarded twenty-four hours a day.'

'I said I believe in coexistence. I didn't say I was a simpleton. These savages respect only one thing: strength. I show them that I have it.'

Angel's route led him across flat scrubland, its grass burned brittle by the sun's relentless assault. He made a mental note of its expanse. He had another five miles to go, he reckoned. It was already appreciably warmer, the bright copper disc of the sun beginning its long trajectory from east to west across the burning sky. His exposed skin tingled. Later, if he remained in the sun naked, it would start to glow, and by nightfall he would have a bad sunburn. On the second day, it would turn to molten agony.

Away off to his left he could see the low line of trees behind which lay the Comanche village. Beyond it to the northeast he could just see the faint yellow-white line that indicated the edge of the desert. The whole valley was a jumble of contradictions, trees growing at the edge of desert, swamp at the feet of lava beds. He had asked his captor about that.

'It is simple,' Nix explained. 'The basic necessity is, of course, water. Give the land enough water, and things will grow. Starve it, and it turns rapidly to desert. Everything else is merely a matter of degree, is it not? I have provided water in certain areas, controlled in certain ways. I control the environment. I designed it myself. Basically it is a circulating system: the well would not provide enough water for it to do as I wish otherwise. Thus the trees which shade the Comanche camp, the pool which supplies their water, are part of this expensive system. They know it. It is a useful reminder of my power, for I have the ultimate deterrent in my hands. One turn of a tap, and their life-support systems will begin to wither.'

'You enjoy playing God?' Angel asked bitingly.

'I am not playing, Angel,' Nix said. 'As you will discover tomorrow.'

'They ought to put you away,' Angel said. 'They ought to lock you up for good in a room with rubber-lined walls. You're sick, Hecatt. Sick in the head!'

'Ah,' Nix smiled. 'You are trying to provoke me again. I've told you, it won't work, Angel. I can wait until morning. Then I will begin to enjoy my revenge. You will be an adversary worthy of the trouble I have taken to prepare this valley. Hunting you down will be a pleasure.'

'Watch out you don't choke on it.'

Nix had looked at Angel reflectively for a moment, the way a parent will look at a child to remind it that it may be going too far with a tantrum. Then he smiled a broad smile. 'Do you know the works of Bacon?' he asked.

'What?'

'Francis Bacon, 1561 to 1626. A contemporary of Shakespeare.'

'I know that. What about him?'

'It was he who said "Hope is a good breakfast, but it is a bad supper",' Nix quoted, and Satan himself could not have had a more malicious gleam in his eyes.

Angel reached his marker.

He had come into the valley knowing rather more about it than he had told Nix, and prepared for several eventualities, one of which was capture. He made a cache for the weapons he had in his rucksack very early on, burying his weapons in a tarp wrapper lightly wiped with gun oil. He lined up a peak on the eastern horizon with a low-lying butte that projected into the valley from the south, and along that line laid two sets of pebble arrows, the arrowheads pointing at each other, about a hundred yards apart. Between them a whitened stick laid casually across another to make a cross marked the cache, and Angel trotted up to it eagerly.

As he got nearer he saw something white

fluttering in the faint breeze. It was a piece of paper in a cleft stick planted in the ground where the cache had been. The cache itself was gone, weapons, everything. The cleft stick held a piece of paper, and on the paper was scrawled a message from Hercules Nix: DO YOU TAKE ME FOR A FOOL?

Frank Angel stood in the bright morning sun, his shoulders slumped in defeat. He looked back across the bare valley to where the *hacienda* lay like a dark smudge at the foot of the folded slopes of the Burros and imagined Nix standing on one of the guard towers, watching through his telescope, smiling like a fox in a chicken coop.

'Bastard!' Angel shouted. He shook his fist in the direction of the stockade, kicked angrily at the turned earth which had concealed his weapons and hidden food. 'Double-crossing bastard!' He made a production out of it, his strung-out curses floating away on the heedless wind. Then, as if coming to a decision, he set off away from his cache toward the northwest, heading for the stand of timber in which the Comanche village lay hidden. He walked slowly, shoulders hunched, his whole bearing that of a man stunned, dejected, defeated. In his mind's eye, he pictured Nix watching and smiling in triumph.

He sure as hell hoped he was, anyway.

EIGHT

Nix led out his men.

There was a small smile of anticipation on his face in the faint light of the dawn, the expression of a man on his way to see good friends, drink good wine, enjoying good talk. He sat in the silver-mounted California saddle erect and proud, like a Greek warrior off to the wars. His mount was the black thoroughbred, a product of the racing stables of Virginia, and worth more than all the other horses of the men around Nix. Des Elliott and his men had no such pretensions. They were a killing crew and they looked it. Most of them had Texas saddles with the center-fire rig, and their mounts were the indigenous *mesteño* breed. Mustangs made more sense in this kind of country. They could live off the land, whereas Nix's fiery steed needed corn to eat, and pampering. Nix's ten men envied their leader his horse, while concealing their envy beneath a veil of disdain: that kind of horse couldn't take punishment. They were kitted out for war.

From Nix's armory, each man had drawn an almost-new Winchester .44-40, one of the new 1873 models. Nix left the choice of sidearms to the individual, and their choice was as varied and murderous as they were. Here a Smith & Wesson American, there a Schofield, a Remington .44. One of Elliott's riders sported a clumsy-looking pair of Starr Army double-actions, but most of them carried the first choice of the paid gun, the short-barreled Colt Peacemaker, chambered for the ammunition the Winchesters used. They were ugly but effective guns, although there were plenty of other weapons to back them if need be. Pocket pistols, Derringers, knives – one man even had a Barns boot pistol, stuck into the top of his boot. He boasted that he'd once used it to stop a train: standing in front of the locomotive and firing the gun head-on at it.

There was little conversation.

Nix's men were already well-drilled in the routine for scouring the valley. Each took a route angled slightly from the almost due north line that Nix rode, with Des Elliott on his left and Bob Dirs, a tow-haired killer from the High Hoban country, on his right. The skull-faced Hisco kicked his mustang into movement, and Barnfield loped out alongside him. They would ford the river and scour the western side of the valley. The rest followed suit, each angling away from the other, fanning across the width of the valley, and nothing in his mind except locating the quarry and picking up the $500 bonus that Nix paid to the man who first found the prey. Five hundred bucks, plus a month away from the valley – that was the kind of motivation Des Elliott's bar-scourings understood. You could wear out your balls in San Antone or Fort Worth if you had that much scratch in your jeans. So they moved steadily, carefully, searching each gully or clump of shrubs, each scatter of rock that might conceal a man.

At each intersection of their chosen paths were rendezvouses. These were rigidly observed, for obvious reasons. If the quarry took out one, or even two of his pursuers soundlessly, their failure to appear at the meeting point would immediately alert the others, and also pinpoint the quarry's location.

Hume Cameron was the favorite.

The predawn briefing had been to the

point and succinct. The last sighting of Angel had been inside the segment Cameron would be covering. Now in the bright morning sunlight he reined in his horse on the fold of a long rise. Away off to his right he could see Nige Hollis working toward the San Miguels. Hollis's paint pony was easy to spot. There was no sign of Mike Hythe. Cameron guessed he was probably checking out the blind canyon. He hitched his hip around on the saddle, stretched his legs in the wooden stirrups. The horse tossed its head and blew through its nose, the bit clunking between its teeth.

Off to his right, Cameron could see a scatter of rounded boulders beside the trail. None of them looked big enough to hide a man. There wasn't enough cover for a jackrabbit, he decided, gigging the horse forward. He thought about Margarita, that little filly he'd met up with in the Eldorado Saloon in San Antone. Dark, she was, with scarlet lips and a waist you could span with your hands. He thought of all the days and nights he could spend with her if he had five hundred dollars. He imagined himself lying in a bed, and Margarita leaning over him naked, her soft breasts warm on his chest. It was as good a thought to die on as any.

Angel didn't give Cameron the ghost of a chance.

He had used an old Apache trick. What the Apache did was to lightly oil their bodies and then roll in the dust until they were coated with it all over. Then they put a large stone on the ground and lay across it, so that their back, with its coating of dust and dirt, looked exactly like a rounded rock. Head, hands, feet were buried in soft dirt, the way a child 'buries' another in the sand. Ten feet away, they would be invisible. Apaches trained themselves to remain immobile over long periods, still and silent as the stones they were imitating, only their watching eyes moving. When the moment was right, they exploded into killing action.

Cameron saw the sudden movement and jerked reflexively on his reins, snatching for the sixgun at his side while his bewildered eyes registered that fact that one of the rocks beside him had come to life, but he was as good as dead by then. The unerringly thrown knife blinked once in the sunlight as it turned in flight, and then buried itself with a soft *thwack!* below the righthand hinge of Cameron's jaw.

The strange, foreign rigidity of steel inside the body is unlike any other hurt. A man can be hit by one, or two or even more bullets, and still manage to continue, to complete his original intention. He can still strike out, still get off his horse, still pull his gun, still fight – bullets or not. Somehow the long, grating slide of the knife blade seems to cut more than flesh, muscle, nerve end, seems to make an aperture out of which the man's sap flows. He does not fight, doesn't strike back. Instead, he is paralyzed by the alien steel in him, as Cameron was. His eyes protruded and he tried to scream, his body overreacting in panic, hastening the work of the weapon in his throat. His body lurched backward in the saddle as he plucked at it with flayed hands which welled blood that joined the awful gouting spurt that leaped suddenly from the severed carotid artery. He crashed from the back of the horse, legs kicking high, still plucking at the weapon in his throat. Finally he got it out and when he did an arc of blood leaped six feet from the wound, while Cameron's body spasmed in the uncaring dust. He was dead in moments, and Frank Angel looked down at the blood already disappearing in the greedy sand, his face without expression. He was not ashamed of the way he'd taken Cameron. He had no qualms about using every dirty trick in the book, and a few that weren't – as long as they worked.

He quickly cleaned himself off and dressed. Picking up Cameron's flat-crowned sombrero, he swung aboard his horse. The animal was still jumpy, shying from the smell of blood, but it quieted as soon as Angel clamped his legs around it. Horses sense very quickly if the rider knows how to control them or not; only inadequate riders get thrown. Now Angel kicked the horse into a walk across the burning land, heading in the direction Cameron had been following before he had taken him off the horse. The two riders who had separated and gone on the northerly tack were almost out of sight, away over toward the line of trees that sheltered the Comanche camp. The one who had headed to Cameron's southern side was up ahead and to Angel's right, turning his horse further southward. He had to be going to meet the fourth rider, Angel decided, the one who'd gone into the blind canyon. He scanned the land ahead. At the foot of the San Miguels lay a long finger of rock that poked out on to the flat plain, forming a halfway point between the edge of the burned scrubland and the shaly beginnings of the desert. Here, the effects of Nix's controlled irrigation petered out, thinned too much to aid growth so that the land became worthless almost immediately. He aimed the horse at the finger of rock. Just move on, he told himself, and see what happens. His guess was that the two riders to his south would move up along the wall of the San Miguels and bisect his path. That way all the land in the arc would have been checked. Mentally, he acknowledged Nix's methods, the planning behind them. It was only because he had been prepared for the man's cunning that he still had a chance of survival.

He was not one of Hercules Nix's rabbits.

The quarry Nix had hunted in his valley had been like men in a poker game who don't know that the tin-horn has marked the cards. Prepared by Welsh Al for the surveillance and the counterchecks, Angel came better prepared, better informed. Knowing he was watched, he had given Nix something to find. He'd buried in the cache that Nix had found a 'survival kit' of a Winchester '73, a Peacemaker with a 4¾-inch barrel, ammunition, rough, penciled maps which he had carefully made inaccurate enough. A waterbottle and some strips of jerky. A compass, a knife, a loop of raw-hide rope. Hercules Nix had located the cache without trouble, of course, it was for that reason that Angel had performed his pantomime at the scene, hoping – feeling pretty certain, actually – that Nix was watching and gloating. That might make Nix a little less careful, and any advantage was one Angel could use. He waited for night before he moved back to the blind canyon through which he had descended into the valley. Here, behind high shoulders of rock screened from the sight of the *hacienda*, he had left his real survival kit. There was a second set of the black leather pants, a woolen shirt, his own mule-ear boots with the socks stuffed inside them. Belt, holster, ammunition, his own seven-inch barreled Peacemaker, the one he'd bought for seventeen dollars direct from the Colt factory at Paterson, New Jersey. Also in the little trench were one or two other items he had asked the Armorer at the Justice Department to put together for him. That dour individual had scanned Angel's handwritten list without any expression, sucking at the stem of a battered old briar for a while before commenting.

'Ye're planning to declare war on someone, then?' he asked finally.

'You could say that,' Angel replied, 'and not be far wrong.'

'Aye,' the Armorer said. 'Well, this lot could make it an interestin' one.'

He'd done everything Angel had asked, and – as usual – a lot more effectively, and on a smaller scale, than anyone had any right to hope. The Armorer had reduced Angel's needs to fit a simple miniature rucksack through which a belt threaded. The whole thing was maybe eighteen inches wide, six deep, the same height. It sat comfortably in the small of the back, in no way interfering with Angel's access to his sixgun. In it were salt tablets, concentrate of chocolate and glucose, a waterskin – more than enough food for a man to survive several days if he had to. Angel had told the Armorer that four days' provisions would be enough. If he wasn't out of the hole in four days, he never would be.

There were some other things in the backpack, things he'd need later if his plans worked. There was a formidable-looking Bowie knife in a sheath which he had strapped onto his own belt. His own throwing knives, made for him by that same armorer a long time ago, were in their hiding place between the inner and outer lining of his boots, their 'mule-ear' pull-on loops serving to conceal the slightly protruding hafts. It was one of these Solingen steel blades that had let the life out of Hume Cameron.

Away off to his right he saw the two Nix riders signal to each other that all was well. They joined up and loped toward a point ahead of Angel, the foot of the long spur of the mountain. He shifted slightly in the saddle and talked Cameron's horse into a faster walk. He didn't want to be seen to be moving faster, but he wanted to get to the rocks before the two Nix riders. The horse picked up its feet, ears pricking. Some animals respond to the whip, others to the word. This was one of the latter, and Angel nodded. Looked like he was going to make it there in time. Odds of a dozen to one were great in story books, but in real life they were too damned high, and he had to try and whittle them down some. He also had to do it in silence. One shot would bring the rest of the gang lally-hooting to the scene, and he wasn't quite ready for that yet. Stalking men like an Apache might not be very sporting, but this crew didn't merit anything better. He had no sympathy for them. He did not give a damn for anything except the knowledge that if he didn't kill them they would as sure as hell kill him, very dead. Which was no damned option. Sliding Cameron's Winchester out of its scabbard, he moved toward the rendezvous where Death sat waiting and grinning in anticipation.

NINE

He let them get quite close.

Cameron's horse was cropping contentedly at the sparse dry grass growing in the cool shadows of the rock outcropping, reins trailing, when Hollis and Mike Hythe rode up.

'Hume?' Hollis called. He pulled his mount to a stop and piled off, kicking up dust as he scuffed across the open space formed by the half circle of rocks. 'Where the hell are you, anyways?'

He looked at Hythe, who shrugged. 'Mebbe he's takin' a leak,' Hythe said, but the words were not properly out before the solid dead silence of the place registered simultaneously on both of them and their faces changed, drastically, as if someone had pulled a plug and their expressions had drained out. Hollis turned toward his partner, lifting a hand and opening his mouth to say something. As he did the first of Frank Angel's arrows drove like a striking cobra into his body, making a wicked, heavy sound as it burst through him and out of his back, smashing him down to the earth, legs kicking high and a thin scream of shocked agony coming from him like a freed ghost. Hythe started for his gun in the same moment that Hollis moved, but he wasn't anywhere near fast enough. You had to be damned fast to outdraw a man who knew how to use a bow and arrow, and Hythe didn't even know where Angel was. A good man could nock and fire off his deadly shafts at least as fast and sometimes even faster than another could thumb back the hammer of a sixgun and fire it.

Angel was a damned good man with every weapon there was.

The Justice Department Armorer had spent a lot of time on the bow and arrows Angel was using. He had made the bow little more than three feet long, two sections that slid into the handgrip, all of it made of laminated steel shafts flattened and joined, strung with a fine-tensioned wire covered with gutta percha. The arrows were of the same lightweight steel tubing and the result was a weapon that could drive the steel shafts through a three-inch block of hardwood at twenty yards. The Armorer had frowned a little over the design Angel had specified for the arrowheads with their wicked barbs, but he'd done it. Mike Hythe looked down at the shaft in his chest as if surprised, reeling back off his horse and going down into the dirt with a flurry that raised dust. He was all the way to the edge of dead, but somehow he floundered to his feet and yanked the ridiculous-looking Barns boot pistol out of his boot, laying it across his blood-soaked forearm. Angel's third arrow was already in the air, but Hythe yanked on the trigger even as the shaft tore out his throat and spun him thrashing to the ground. The pistol made a noise like a thunderclap, reverberating off the rocks above the killing ground as the .50 caliber bullet whined away into infinity.

'Damnation!' Angel gritted silently.

The whole idea of his weapons had been their silence: he had hoped for more advantage. Nix and his riders would have certainly heard the boom of the Barns pistol, and the sound of a shot would mean only one thing to them. Angel ran down from his hiding place in the rocks, not looking at the sprawled dead men. Moving quickly, he laced the reins of their horses to the saddle pommels and slapped the animals on their haunches. They moved off smartly, heading home. Angel didn't think there was much chance of Nix falling for such an ancient wheeze, but even if one man was detached to check the dust, that was one man less to fight now.

He cast a rapid glance at the edge of the scrubland, and thought he could see a faint plume of dust near the line of trees, heading in his direction. He swung into the saddle and kicked the mustang into a run. He would be cutting it damned fine, but there was still a decent chance that he could make his destination. He leaned forward and talked to the horse, and once again, it responded with more speed.

Then he saw the second cloud of dust.

In the opening stages of the chase, Hercules Nix always took the center line. His usual practice – which his men knew well – was to ride due north with Elliott and Dirs until they reached the far side of the Comanche woods. There, Elliott would swing west toward the river, Dirs to the east and the desert's edge. Nix would remain in the center.

Thus it was that when they heard the shots, Dirs was the nearest to Angel's position, Elliott farthest away. Only waiting to ensure that Nix was swinging his horse around, Dirs thundered off southward, heading for the wide opening between the spur of the San Miguels to his left, and the edge of the woods on his right. He did not look back, knowing that Nix and Elliott would be following his dust. He narrowed his eyes to peer into the rush of the wind and saw a lone rider heading at an angle across his path to the right. Some distance further to the right – southwest – he saw two other riders heading at an angle to bisect the arc drawn between the lone rider and himself. It had to be Angel! Dirs's lips stretched back off his teeth and he grinned like a Death's head into the wind. The quarry was heading into the thin scree at the edge of the woods, and now Dirs saw that the other two riders pursuing Angel were Ricky Cross and a man known only as The Major, who was reputed to be on the run from the Army. He felt a surge of triumph. They had Angel cold. If he turned north, he'd blunder right into the Comanche camp, and they'd likely kill him on sight. Even if they didn't, they'd kick seven different kinds of shit out of him before handing him over to Hercules Nix. If Angel turned right around and ran south, he'd be out in the open. In the unlikely event they didn't run him down out there, he'd come up finally against the impassable barrier of the southern mountains with no place to hide. These thoughts made Bob Dirs grin like a wolf spotting a lamb with a broken leg, and he larruped his horse with the reins.

'Got you, you sonofabitch!' he shouted, thinking of five hundred dollars.

Angel got into the trees maybe a quarter of a mile before his pursuers, but it was enough. They couldn't move among the trees as fast as he, who knew nothing lay ahead of him. They would have to come in slowly, carefully. It was cool and shady under the trees. The horse moved soundlessly on the thick carpet of leaf mold, through great swathes of shadow and between dusty columns of slanting sunshine. Here and there lay great gray moss-covered rocks that looked like sleeping dinosaurs. He moved as fast as he dared, trying to be silent. He had only a little time, and he had to make it pay. By the time

Cross and The Major eased through the trees into the clearing he had chosen, Angel was good and ready.

Cross saw him first and gave a yell of triumph.

'Hold it right there!' he shouted. 'Hold it!'

He froze as he saw that Angel had a Winchester leveled at him. The quarry was standing in the center of a small glade, back to a big rock. He looked like he was ready to fight it out, and Cross didn't want to shoot him down before Nix got on the scene. He turned toward the Major. The Major winked. Cross grinned, and nodded. They knew that Bobbie Dirs had worked around behind the quarry. He'd make a move in a moment, and then the game could begin. Nix didn't mind what they did to the quarry as long as they didn't wound him so badly he was no more fun. Meanwhile, they had him. There was no damned hurry at all.

The tableau was like something painted, frozen. Angel there in the glade, back protected by the rock, Winchester leveled at the two dismounted men. He could almost hear the seconds ticking past, and willed the man behind him to make his move.

Almost as if anxious to oblige him, Dirs got himself firmly set in the saddle, and eased his Winchester from the scabbard. He was about fifty feet away from the glade, and when he was ready he gave the high sign to his two comrades and dug his spurs in hard. The horse buck-jumped into full gallop, and as he started moving, Dirs reversed the carbine so that the barrel was in his hands, swinging the weapon like a polo stick. He had a savage grin of exultation on his face and there ought to have been no damned chance for Frank Angel in this world.

Then Dirs hit the wire.

It was practically invisible, stretched tightly from tree to tree and forming a square around Angel's position, at approximately the height of the chest of a man on horseback. It was top quality steel leader, bought at Angel's request from the New York sporting goods firm of Calhoun and Witherspoon, on Third Avenue. It was normally used by that strange breed who fish the ice-blue waters of the Gulf Stream for marlin, and sailfish, and even shark; and it had a minimum breaking strain of four hundred pounds. The way that Angel had rigged it, stretched twang-tight like a guitar string, it formed a cutting edge as effective as a cheese wire and Dirs's neck hit the wire while he was at full gallop.

What happened next paralyzed Cross and The Major in horror. Dirs's Winchester exploded harmlessly at the reflex pull of his dying finger and the slug whined away somewhere, harmless. The two paid guns watched transfixed by the sight of the specter rushing toward them, a headless thing that spurted blood as it reeled out of the saddle while its severed head bounded across the clearing like a rolled rock and disappeared from sight among the trees.

Cross gave a formless shout and yanked out his Starr Army pistols, falling sideways to the ground as he did. The Major was already on the ground, body neatly arranged in the lying-load position, legs askew and feet flattened inside-down, firing useless shots at the place where Angel had been.

'Behind the rock!' Cross hissed. 'He must be behind the rock!'

The Major gave an enormous shrug. He was not given to talking much. Besides, Nix and the others would be here in a few minutes. Why take chances? Cross made a furious gesture. *Go around that way*, it said. *Behind him*.

The Major's lip curled and he made a signal of his own, less military but none the less perfunctory. Cross scowled across the yards that separated them, and then wormed off into the undergrowth, his whole posture plain with his message: damn you, I'll do it myself.

The Major watched him go, impassively. They had all the time in the world. What Cross hoped to prove he could not imagine. Angel had killed Bobbie Dirs but that wasn't the end of the world. The others must be only a few minutes away at most. He eased his left leg into a more comfortable position, and relaxed.

Ricky Cross was anything but relaxed. He was killing mad. Bobbie Dirs had been a pal of his, and the way this bastard Angel had killed him was, well, butchery. Cross felt even worse because, somehow, he'd stood there and let Angel pull it. He peered through the screening leaves. Nothing moved anywhere, unless you counted the normal chatter of birds, the soft buzz of insects. He eeled further forward. Pretty soon now he would be able to see in back of the big rock behind which Angel had taken shelter. He had one Starr in each hand, using his elbows for forward leverage. Keeping his head low, he advanced silently, every sense tuned, every nerve taut, ready for anything.

Anything except what happened.

TEN

Cross lifted his head.

He was lying at the foot of a long, gentle slope gullied by runoffs, shaded by wide-armed trees. He could have been the last man alive in the world, so quiet was it. He raised himself a little higher and as he did, the rolling head of Bobbie Dirs bumped down the slope, hit a hummock, bounced into his chest and fell at his feet. Dirs's still-surprised eyes glared sightlessly at him. Without volition, Cross screamed.

The sound was exactly like the sound that a pig makes when it is being slaughtered. The butcher puts the long, narrow-bladed knife into the animal's throat almost before it knows it, and it is as the little mouth of death opens in its flesh that the pig gives off its shriek. It is a sound that cannot be forgotten by anyone who has ever heard it. Cross was still making the awful sound as he scrambled to his feet, mindless, blind-eyed, desperate only to get away from the horrible thing that lay inches before his eyes.

He got six yards before Angel cut him down.

Cross blundered like a stampeding buffalo out of the clinging undergrowth and burst into the open, his eyes glazed with terror, then stopped. His head turned to the right and then the left, like a man unsure of his route, and in the same moment, the realization came into his expression that he was totally at risk. He was still digesting that realization when the fourth of Angel's steel arrows drew a line of shimmering silver across the shadowed clearing. It hit Cross in the temple and he was flung like a rag doll against an angled birch that quivered and shed leaves as the dead weight smashed into it. Cross kicked twice in reflex, the staggered barbs of the arrowhead protruding bloodily from his right eye socket, his brain split by the irresistible force of the driven shaft.

'Four,' Frank Angel muttered, easing back below the fallen log on which he had rested his left elbow for certain aim. He glanced up at the patch of sky he could see through the screening curtain of leaves. In another couple of hours it would be dark. The air smelled soft, damp; there might be rain on the way.

He lay motionless as a hunting puma.

There is enormous discipline in remaining completely still, totally silent, especially when you are being hunted. Not many men can do it. They fall prey to the temptation to move slightly, to peer from their place of concealment, see if anyone is coming, check that all is well. It is often a fatal error, and Angel did not make it. He knew he was well hidden, for he had chosen his hiding place with extreme care, using the open space of the clearing to make a long leap into the center of an abundant stand of chest-high ferns growing beneath the trees. He landed like a cat, then moved very carefully sideways about ten yards, lost in the tangled profusion of the plants. He was to all intents and purposes invisible, and he lay like a fallen tree, concentrating upon inner silence as he had been taught by the little Korean, Kee Lai.

You must learn to control all of yourself, mind and body together. Once you have this control, you can do anything. Observe the hunted things. See how they protect themselves, watch how they hide. They become one with the trees that shelter them, the earth that shields them, the plants that surround them. Do this also. Listen to the turning of the earth, the passing of the clouds, the coming and going of the wind. When you truly hear all these, nothing else can escape your ears.

The earth smelled strong and rich. He heard birds moving in the branches overhead, the soft sigh of the breeze amid the bright leaves. Small insects buzzed. Ants marched erratically across his spread hands. Watching ants you feel like God, he thought. Are we to them as God is to us? We casually step on a cluster of ants, destroy with a casual swipe one which dares to touch our precious flesh, drive our horses through their intricately built nests. Are we to them what accidents, murders, earthquakes are to us? Are God's moods as random as ours?

He heard a twig snap, off to his right.

'Major!' a voice hissed. 'Major, you there?'

'Here,' another voice whispered, somewhere behind Angel's position. 'That you, Elliott?'

'Yeah,' Elliott said. 'You see anything?'

'No sign of him. He killed Ricky, though.'

'I seen it.'

Angel heard the thick, clumsy crackle of a man moving through the undergrowth. About fifty yards away, he reckoned, and off to the right. Too far, he thought, feeling coolness in the air. Night was on its way.

'Where's the boss?' he heard the one called

Major hiss. In his mind's eye, he saw them hunkered together somewhere. That was the reason for the crackle of movement, Elliot shifting his position to join Major. They would be behind a tree or a big rock, eyes wary, nerves tense, guns ready, sweating. Let them sweat: that was part of his psychology. The first principal of guerilla fighting was to get your enemy off balance, nervous. The guerilla fights the war of the flea, and his larger enemy suffers the disadvantages of the dog: too much to defend, too small, ubiquitous, and agile an enemy to come to grips with. Most of Hercules Nix's previous victims had been hyped into playing the game by Nix's rules: they had simply run, and thus been easy to take. None had used Angel's hit-and-run technique, giving Nix's killers no time to settle to their work. They wouldn't have the stomach for fighting the war of the flea. Angel smiled in the dark coolness of his hiding place.

Hercules Nix was not a fool. He knew about the war of the flea, and he knew, as soon as Elliott gave him a situation report, that Angel had chosen to fight it. He smiled at the man's determination and skill. He had badly underestimated his quarry, and it had cost him four men. Hercules Nix cared less than nothing about that, of course. He paid his killers to take risks. The buzzards took care of those who fell. As for himself, he had revised his plans, for he had no intention of playing into Angel's hands. He called his men back out of the trees, and sent the Major across to the barracks at the Portal. There were half a dozen men there, and Barnfield and the skull-faced Hisco would have completed their sweep of the western side of the valley by now. Two men would be enough to hold the entrance road; the others could be here by first light.

'What you got in mind?' Des Elliott asked.

Nix smiled, the smile of a man still supremely confident. He waved his hand at the trees. Darkness was coming slowly down from the San Miguels, spreading across the floor of the valley, stealing away the distances.

'He's in there somewhere,' he said. 'Correct?' Elliott nodded; it was hardly a revelation.

'What will he do? Lie low, or cut and run?'

'He might run for it. Use darkness to make a break.'

'Not this one,' Nix said, emphatically. 'He *wants* us to go in there and look for him. That way he could take us one at a time.

We'd never even see him. Our advantages are numbers, firepower. In there we lose them.'

'Agreed,' Elliott said. 'So how do we take him?'

'We have to get him out in the open, where he can't use that incredible bow or crossbow or whatever it is. Where whatever other tricks he has up his sleeve won't work.'

'Terrific,' Elliott said. 'How do we pull that with a dozen men?'

'We don't,' Nix said dreamily. 'Have you ever heard how they hunt lion?'

'Uh? Hunted what?'

'Lion,' Nix repeated. 'In Africa. It's a very simple system, practically infallible. They get all the people of the village to act as beaters. They take drums and buckets and anything that will make a noise, and they go into the long grass where the lion hides, banging and shouting and whistling, dozens and dozens of them – far too many for Simba to attack, even if he wanted to. He has no choice left. If he lies where he is, one of them will find him, and the hunters will come. He drops back to a new hiding place. But the beaters move on, inexorably. Again, Simba moves, but now he is running out of hiding places. What shall he do? Behind him are the beaters, sounding like all the devils in hell on a holiday. Ahead of him is the empty open plain, with no long grass to shield him.'

'And then?'

'He moves out into the open. And the real hunters are waiting to kill him.'

'I'm beginnin' to get your drift,' Elliott grinned. 'You're goin' to use the Injuns as beaters, right?'

'Right,' Nix said. 'We'll get all the women and kids at the southern side of the woods. At first light, they move in, one long line of them!'

'And we'll be waiting,' Elliott said, showing his teeth in a feline grin.

'Correct,' Nix said. The way to combat the war of the flea was to shear the dog. He saw himself sitting on the black stallion at the northern edge of the forest as the Indians worked their way through the woods. He imagined the panicked figure of the hunted man bursting through the tangled undergrowth and then, left with no choice, heading out into the open where the hunters waited. He saw himself riding the man down, white glimpse of face beneath the thundering hoofs, despairing shout of pain. Like shooting fish in a barrel, he thought, with a wicked smile of anticipation. They had Mister Angel on a plate.

ELEVEN

Night fell like a blanket.

Now, and only now, did Frank Angel rise from his chilly lair to stretch cramped muscles, speed slowed circulation. It was somewhere between unlikely and impossible that Nix would send his men in after the quarry in the dark, but he wasn't about to take that fact for granted. He tried to put himself in Nix's place, think what the big man might do next.

When you're alone and hunted, there is nobody to help.

You can guess what your pursuer may do, hope you are right. It's not a lot of help, because you only get one chance to be wrong. Your pursuer can make as many errors as he likes, given an endless supply of men and money and time. He can try again and again and again. Not you. One false step, one overlooked factor, and you are dead meat. So Angel made no hasty moves. Ignoring the gnawing pangs of hunger in his belly, he sat beneath a tree and considered his options. There was no easy way out of the forest. It was big enough to hide in, but it was also small enough to encircle. If he were Nix, he would use his men like a trail boss would use them, treating the forest as the herd. The men would ride around it in pairs, like night riders, always within earshot of each other. In the night silence, any movement would be quite easy to detect. He had long since abandoned the thought of using the horse, which must still be loose somewhere in the woods. They would hear his approach half a mile away if he tried to break out on horseback. So what to do? He considered some other possibilities, rejecting them as he did. Playing sniper; lying low and waiting to see what Nix would do; even firing the woods and using the flames to conceal his escape. None of them was feasible.

Attack, they said, was the best form of defense.

He got to his feet and moved silently through the trees, careful not to startle any foraging night animal, moving northward until his nostrils were assailed by the stink of the Comanche encampment. Then he paused to take his bearings. A gently sloping declivity lay before him, at the bottom of which lay a lapping pool of water, perhaps thirty feet across and twice as many long. Its shelving banks were trampled clay, denuded of bushes and grass by the endless procession of moccasined feet to the water's edge. About fifty yards from the edge of the water was a lazily flickering fire, near which several men slept on blankets.

The stink was strong enough to slice.

Comanches had no concept of hygiene, and never washed except during ceremonial purifications. Normally, they simply pulled up their stakes and quit a campsite once it began to smell too badly. This protected haven was too good to quit, but that did not mean they took care not to defoul it. A long line of teepees faced the water, and behind that another and then another. Between them was a wide space, like a street. The teepees had a four-pole base, twenty-two poles to a frame. Most of them were about fifteen feet high, and of about the same diameter. They took up a lot of space, and to a degree Angel was surprised to see them. It must be the semi-permanent nature of the camp, he thought. Comanches usually slept outdoors in the summer, on light bedding or in brush arbors. They were a strange, outcast race, unlike any of the other Indian tribes. They cared nothing for the symbols of status and bravery that other Plains tribes prized. Comanch' wore no eagle feathers, no war-bonnets, no beaded buckskin. Breechclout and hip-high painted hunting boots were the standard garb of the Comanche fighting man in summer. His status and deeds were recorded upon his war shield, constructed of layered buffalo hide and capable of deflecting a well-aimed arrow at fifty feet. War shields were painted with magic symbols with special meaning for the warrior who carried them; sometimes the teeth of slain bears, horsetails, or human scalps were added. These also demonstrated prowess. Horse tails advertised the owner's skill in that most admired of all Comanche arts, stealing horses.

The shields were a great help to the hidden man, for they told him many things. No warrior ever took his war shield into the teepee, where its medicine might be lessened by contact with people – especially unclean people like women. No woman was allowed near a war shield, much less to touch it. Instead warriors stored their shields at the edge of the camp, or in some central spot. In a sloppy, polluted dump like this, they were leaned against the sides of the teepees, and their presence made it easy for Angel to assess the probable strength of the camp. Fourteen fighting men, and these probably the dregs of the band. The others must be out raiding, and those left behind would be the sick, the wounded, the old. Mostly the sick, Angel thought, smiling without humor. Comanch' were more often out of commission because of their complete ignorance of the most elementary rules of sanitation than because of war wounds. He recalled what one hardbitten cavalryman he knew had called the complaint: the Comanche Two-Step.

He estimated the total number of teepees at around forty-five, moving around the perimeter under the cover of night, using black pools of deeper shadow, ever wary of sleeping curs. Rouse one of those yapping animals, and the camp would be awake in moments. The women would kill you as readily as the men, but they wouldn't be as merciful. He reached the northern edge of the camp and found the horse herd without difficulty. There were about twenty ponies in a rope corral that closed in a smaller, but no less trampled clearing. Further evidence that the warriors in this encampment were second class. Some top war leaders of the Comanche owned as many as fifteen hundred horses, for horse-flesh was the ultimate Comanche status symbol. With the real fighting men away, what was left behind was a sorry-looking lot. He tested the faint breeze and kept upwind of the horses for now. He was near enough for the animals to see him if he moved, and he wanted to let them get accustomed to his presence without detecting his alien smell. If they caught his scent, they would react, and that would bring someone running.

He got some of the food out of his backpack and sat in the darkness trying to make believe it was a medium-rare steak with hashed brown potatoes and fried eggs with a side dish of canned tomatoes. Maybe some sourdough-bread and fresh butter. He thought of his landlady, Mrs Rissick, toiling up the stairs in the house on F Street in Washington, her shopping bag bulging. He thought of ripe Stilton cheese, a good bottle of claret, fresh peaches. He remembered being in the mountains and taking trout from the chattering river, cooking it in a stock of seven parts water, one part vinegar.

He drank some water and stowed away his gear, waiting for the false dawn.

He wondered when the raiding Comanches were due back in the encampment.

Full moon was their favorite time for raiding, and the full moon had waned some nights ago. The Comanches did not like the quarter moon period, for they believed it presaged rain, which made mud and held tracks by which a raiding party could be followed.

Soon it was time, and he stretched his limbs with infinite care. The sharp tang of wood smoke told him the women were already up and about in the camp, and he saluted their industry, for the soft sharp smell of their fires would mask his own alien smell among the horses. Very carefully, he slipped beneath the encircling rope of the corral and laid his hand on one of the mustangs. The animal tensed, its hide bunching as Angel walked his hand along it, softly uttering soothing sounds until he was close to its head.

He laid a gentle hand on the horse's muzzle and put his own head close to that of the animal, blowing gently into its nostrils the way he had once been taught by a Cheyenne horsebreaker named Charlie Steelass. The horse nodded, pushing itself against him. Angel let it, knowing that its smell would mask his own. He moved to its right-hand side. Comanches mounted on the right, Spanish style. Everything they did on horseback, they did Spanish style, for it was from the invading Spanish and their descendants that they had learned how to handle horses, watching and watching with those dark unreadable eyes. Until they learned.

Grasping the mustang's mane, Angel vaulted on to its back. Keeping his hand bunched in its mane, Angel sat immobile as the animal tensed, waiting for him to command it. When he did not, it relaxed, and he let it make its own way to the far side of the corral, milling with the other horses. When it got where he wanted it to be, Angel leaned over and deftly sliced the horsehair rope barring the opening that debauched on the camp. As the strands parted, he rammed his heels into the mustang's ribs and let loose the shrillest Rebel yell he could manage.

The milling herd of horses reacted as if someone had fired a cannon in their midst. They exploded out of the corral and thundered in a panicked tide down the ragged open space that served as the camp's street. In the center of the herd, hanging down the flank of his horse by holding on with right leg and left hand, Comanche style, Angel saw men stumbling out of the teepees, waving and shouting and trying to stop the stampeding herd. Their figures blurred behind the glinting cloud of dust the unshod hoofs had raised, and Angel thought he heard a thin scream as someone went down beneath the slashing feet.

Although he had no great opinion of their intelligence, Angel had put his faith in the memory of the ponies. Horses rarely forgot their training. He had once taken Amabel Rowe riding in a carriage around Central Park in New York. Halfway past the Sheep Meadow, they noticed that the driver was asleep and awakened him, pointing out that nobody was watching the road.

'Well, now, and don't be fright,' said the cabman, whose name was Bernie McGann. 'Sure the horse knows the way.'

Even these half wild mustangs knew the way in and out of the woods in which the encampment lay, and Angel swung up to lie low along his mount's back as the herd crashed through the thin, screening bushes bordering the well-trampled pathway leading out to the open plain. They burst out into the open like a tidal wave.

In the growing half-light, Angel saw two riders off to his left racking their startled horses around and kicking them into a run to head off the widening fan of Comanche ponies. A glance to the right revealed two more riders, but further away, probably too far for it to make any real difference. He unshipped the short bow that he'd looped over his right shoulder. There were only two arrows left, a fact of life he accepted without regret. He had not known what his needs would be: six of the steel shafts had seemed enough to carry when he started out. Every one of them had paid its dues so far.

Angel was no Comanche.

He could not, as they could, hit running quail from horseback with bow and arrow; but he was better than good. Between two strides of the galloping pony, he released the first of his shafts, and using the same optimum moment for aim and accuracy, released the last seconds later. Then he put his head down and concentrated on urging the flying Comanche pony to even greater speed, pointing its head north. When he looked back he saw that one of the pursuing horses was trailing to a riderless halt and the second was down in a thrashing pile, legs striking out in spasms of agony. Looked like he had missed the second man and hit his horse instead. Now he saw the man scrambling to his feet, running away from the gutshot horse toward where his comrade had fallen, and Angel nodded in grim satisfaction. If one of the arrows had hit the fallen man, it didn't make any difference where: he was out of it. The mustang herd was beginning to spread out now, the leaders beginning to mill as they went over the crest of a long bluff that led downward in a long flat slope toward the edge of the scrubland and the beginnings of a stony, brushless stretch of land presaging the desert beyond it. Using hands and heels and voice, Angel urged his own pony on, risking one last look back over his shoulder. The light was much better now, but there were pregnant blue-black clouds low over the mountains and once he thought he saw the flicker of lightning. There were four dark blobs on the darkening land behind him, a couple of miles back. Knowing that Nix had a fine thoroughbred horse, Angel hoped he had a long enough start. Nix's horse could probably outrun everything in Texas if he put his spurs into it. He felt the soft plop of heavy raindrops on his face, and threw back his head to welcome them. Not even Nix's stallion could run fast in a Texas rainstorm. There was more thunder in the sky, awaiting its cue from the lightning. Ahead of him was the long dark line of the swampy jungle around the muddy lake. Once again Angel grinned his cold wolf's grin.

Let them come find him in there.

TWELVE

As he reached the edge of the timber line, the skies opened. The rain came down in a vertical curtain that blotted out light, killed the growing daylight, flattening everything beneath it. It soaked through Angel's clothes in moments, and brought steam from the hot flanks of the gallant little Comanche pony that stood with its head down where Angel had dismounted.

Lightfooted as an Indian, Angel ran through the dank screen of undergrowth, keeping always to the lighter-colored patches of spongy ground he could see. There were often stretches of what looked like firm, verdant ground beneath the trees, but no bushes grew on them and he knew they were purest treachery, swampy layers of grass floating on a base of thick and glutinous mud. Put your full weight on these patches and down you would go, up to the hips or deeper in stinking filth, easy prey for water moccasin or alligator. The tuftier, lighter-colored grass was usually sprinkled about with small shrubs or shoots from seedlings dropped by the trees above, sure sign that there was enough earth to take a man's running weight.

He reckoned he had about ten minutes' start, not more. Four or five minutes for them to cover the distance he'd been ahead, as many again to pile off and decide their next move. They wouldn't come in blind after him, but they had to come in, and they had to come in from the south. If they wanted to get around ahead of him, they would have had to ride all the way back to the dry ford across the river, the only safe way to cross it, then cover the same distance back on the far side to reach the northern edge of the muddy lake. Nix would be too hot to catch him now to split his force. With five men dead and nothing to show for it, he would need some kind of success to show his men. Maybe he would abandon a little of his caution trying to get it.

The rain kept thrashing down against the dense shield of the screening leaves, drowning sound, sensation, everything. Angel changed direction now, moving back toward the east, using every leaf for cover. After a while, he heard the hoarse sound of someone shouting. The rain was easing slightly, and over its steady driving rattle he could hear the eruptive sounds of men slushing through the trees, whacking at the undergrowth with machetes. Peering through the spattering mist of water, Angel saw their dark shapes and the betraying movement of the trees as they passed through. They were in a rough line abreast, twenty or so yards apart, working their way through the undergrowth with the short, wicked machetes in one hand and sixguns in the other. One man was covered in mud, his eyes startling white holes in the running gray mask of filth. He eased backward, heading for the farthest end of the ragged line. He could see no sign of Hercules Nix yet, but in this bad light, in this driving rain, it was hard to identify anyone.

The man at the end of the line was tall and thin, with a hooked nose and a three-day stubble that gave him a wolflike appearance. He sloshed through a sucking trough of seeping muddy water, and threw himself down on a hummock of grass with a disgusted curse, pulling off his boots and draining the gummy water out of them. He still had one of the boots in his right hand when Angel came around the tree behind him.

The man opened his mouth to scream, but he never made it.

Angel's sweet movement was too fast. The man had time to drop his boot, register Angel's presence, and see that Angel had picked up the machete. Then the thick heavy blade sliced his heart in two and pinned the man's contorted body to the heedless trunk of the tree behind him. The scream turned into a choking gurgle and Angel caught the startled shout of the next man up the line as he heard it. He was out of sight when the first of them came at a lumpy run through the swampy muck, and watched as a second man joined him, eyes bulging at the awful sight of their comrade pinned like some strange insect against the hole of the live oak.

'He's killed Levi,' the first man said. Then he shouted the same words at the top of his voice. A voice Angel recognized as Elliott's bounced back through the trees, flattened by the sound of the rain.

'All right!' Elliott yelled. 'Make a half-circle. But don't bunch up, he's probably picking a spot to kill you! Make your half-circle, don't let him get between you!'

The two men looked at each other in sudden panic, and floundered away in opposite directions, moving back to where they could see the others. They were the touch points in the plan, which was that when the quarry was located, the others would swing out to form a wide half-circle. Somewhere inside it would be Angel. Then they would close in on him. It was a good idea, but Angel put a hole in it by removing one of the touch points. Barnfield, the man who'd discovered the dead Levi, was wishing to God he'd stayed up at the Portal instead of rushing out to try and earn Nix's five hundred dollar bonus. His nerve was shot to hell from the sight of seeing Levi nailed to that tree, and he was breathing raggedly, hands dank with sweat even in this strange swampy rain. He jumped every time the leaves in front of him moved. He was so much on edge that when Angel stepped out in front of him, Barnfield stopped dead in his tracks, paralyzed with fear.

He stood like that for perhaps two seconds, but that was enough. Angel was quite ready, his body perfectly set for what he had to do, and even as the croak of alarm was born in Barnfield's suddenly dry throat, Angel's right arm was moving in a horizontal arc that brought the toughened outer edge of his right hand across at a speed that defied sight. It struck Barnfield just below his right ear, and the lanky man went down on his knees in the mud, coordination shot to hell, the sixgun dropping from his nerveless fingers with a muddy plop to sink into the mire. Before the mud had even begun to close over the gun, Angel's body was moving back the way it had turned, his left hand striking Barnfield directly beneath his gathered eye-brows. The force of the blow smashed in the fragile frontal bones of the skull, and Barnfield catapulted back into the bushes, contorted in agony, legs thrashing as a strangulated caw of terror and pain broke from his stunned throat. He thrashed around in the muddy slop like some strange animal with its spine broken, and Angel heard someone shout, then shout again.

'Barney?' the voice called. It broke nervously on the second syllable. When there was no reply, the man blundered nearer, and as if on signal, the pent-up thunder blasted across the iron-gray sky like the veritable wrath of God. There was the sharp electric click of lightning and then the bright copper smell of ozone. The thunder roared and rolled in one long continuously awesome sound that seemed to shake the very earth, and the rain came down with renewed violence, drawing half-white lines across the darker shadows at an angle of eighty degrees, reducing visibility to almost nil faster than it takes to say it.

The man who had shouted out to Barnfield was still shouting, but in the immense roar of unleashed nature, his voice was like that of a cat mewling at Niagara. He blundered right past where his comrade was struggling in the mud, half-conscious, trying blindly to get to his feet. Angel let him go five paces and then broke the dry stick in his hands with a decisive crack. His timing was perfect. The man whirled around, sixgun coming up as Barnfield labored to his feet, reeling forward, a muddy apparition making a senseless sound that brought an instant reflex action from his comrade. He fanned back the hammer in a blur of movement that emptied the sixgun in one long stutter of fire, smashing the lanky Barnfield back down into the glutinous mud, riddled, while the man who had killed him gaped in honor at the fallen body. Barnfield's face was upturned, and the driving rain washed off the mud as the man stood staring at what he had done. He looked from side to side in utter panic.

'Hammond!' someone shouted. 'Where the hell are you?'

'Here,' the thickset one with the gun shouted weakly. Then louder. 'Here! Here! Over here! Barney's dead!'

'Heard shots,' another man panted, splashing into view. He was skeleton-faced, his white hair plastered to his skull. Angel, hidden where he had faded from view as Hammond came on the scene, recognized this one. They called him Hisco.

'D'ya see him?' Hisco asked Hammond.

'No,' Hammond lied. 'Heard the shots, like you. Come a-runnin', but Barney was dead already.'

Hisco turned Barnfield's body slightly with a soggy boot. He grinned, the unfeeling grin of a man who has looked at dead men many times.

'Got enough holes in him to use for a waterin' can,' he said.

'Christ, Hisco,' Hammond said, teeth chattering as if with ague. 'Ain't no call for that sort o' talk!'

'Shit,' Hisco snapped, 'he's just as dead, whatever. Come on, haul your ass!'

He pushed Hammond roughly, indicating that the dumpy man should lead off to the left. Hisco had his own gun out, a silver-plated, scroll-engraved Smith & Wesson .44 with an ivory grip. Pimp's gun, Angel thought, as he moved silently back into the inky shadows. The vicious downpour had now eased into a steady torrent, and the constant spatter of the rain upon the broad-leafed trees and bushes drowned any small noises that he might have made. He eased further back. Where was Hercules Nix?

Almost as if to answer his question, he came upon two more of Nix's men, squatting in a dry patch beneath a huge tree. Angel drew back into hiding, taking perverse pleasure in watching the men's misery as they tried to light sodden cigarettes. Eventually they threw down the soaked papers and shredded Durham in disgust.

'Waal, God damn everything to hell-and-go-on,' one of them drawled with the unmistakable softness of the Southerner. 'Ya cain't even git a smoke in thisyere gumbo.'

'Prob'ly just as well,' the other said. 'Don't figger it's a good idee. Let's git movin' in case the boss comes on us.'

'Needn't worry none, boy,' the Southerner said. 'He's gone on back to the edge o' the trees. Claims he's goin' to see if he can spot this Angel feller from out thar. We up to our asses in liquid shit, an' he's done pulled back to drah land.'

'You better not let him hear you talkin' like that, Mike. He's gutted men for less.'

'Fust ketch yore possum,' Mike said with an unrepentant grin. 'Lissen, Watson, thisyere Angel fella ain't no pussycat. Anyone kills off seven good men like he's done don't hardly do to mess with. I ain't gittin' any dinged closer to him than I got to, Mister Hercules Nix or not!'

'What you plannin' to do, Mike?' Watson asked.

'Take 'er easy, boy,' Mike said. 'Thassall, take 'er easy. Just hang on back aways, don't be no eager beaver. That Angel feller out thar, he's plannin' on killin' ever' one of us as gits too close. I figger, what the hell, don't git too close, raht?'

'Mike,' Watson grinned. 'You're a crafty sonofabitch.'

'Dooley,' Mike grinned sourly back, 'ain't it the awful truth?'

Giving his comrade a light punch on the shoulder, Watson pushed off into the soaked maze of brush and undergrowth. After a few seconds, the one called Mike shrugged and followed suit. Angel watched them go, counting slowly. When he reached five hundred, he slid off silently in their wake. He was behind them now, and he intended to make the very best use of his advantage.

But he reckoned without The Major.

THIRTEEN

Nobody knew The Major's real name.

Nobody, that is, except the man himself, and The Major wasn't talking. In fact, as any of the men who rode for Hercules Nix would have testified, getting information out of The Major was a bit like collecting the teeth of live sharks: damned interesting, maybe, but the best way there was to get your head bitten off. Since Nix cared nothing about a man's pedigree, but only his abilities, The Major had never been required to give one. His case-hardened comrades soon grew tired of shouting 'Hey, you!' after him, and dubbed him for his ramrod bearing and staccato speech.

Actually he'd never been more than a Sergeant in the 11th Ohio Cavalry, but if they wanted to think he'd been an officer, let them. He didn't figure it was any of their business that he'd done three five-year hitches, the first starting when he was so desperate for work that he'd been peeling potatoes in the kitchen of the Grand Union Hotel in Chicago for three cents an hour. He began his second hitch in 1864, not that he was given any damned choice: the country was in the throes of the War. They paid a man sixteen dollars a month, less dockings, for the privilege of sending him out every day, every week, every month for the best part of five years to get his fool head blown off. After the War, to show its deep gratitude to the men who had saved the Union, Congress reduced that to thirteen dollars, and substituted Sioux and Cheyenne for Johnny Rebs. Forty-three cents a day: it wasn't enough to keep a man in underwear, and he ended his second hitch so deep in debt he had to sign on again. He owned the sutlers and the whores and the off-limits saloons and the loan sharks who'd pay you out ten dollars in midmonth and charge you two dollars a week interest on it, then let it run up so high you ended up being a virtual slave to them. When he made it to Sergeant, The Major put the screws on the enlisted men even tighter than they'd been put on him when he was in the ranks. He bled them all dry, and when he came to the end of his third hitch, he told the Army what it could do with its McLellan saddle and its blue serge and brass buttons, its stinking barracks and its slack-bellied 'washer-women.' Taking his hoarded gold and his mustering-out pay, he quit Fort Riley and hit Abilene like a raider. He didn't draw a sober breath for nearly two weeks, in which time he figured he'd laid every two-dollar whore in town. The Major was interested in quantity, not quality. With what money he had left, he got into a poker game run by an expert. The dandified, ruffle-shirted tinhorn who dealt took The Major for every cent he had. The Major called him a cheat, which he was, and the gambler shook a nasty little Derringer out of his sleeve but he stopped doing that when The Major rammed six inches of cold steel bayonet into the man's belly and left him squirming on the sawdust floor of the Alamo with black blood coming out of his mouth. The Major quit town before the man's friends could find him and lynch him, and found out a few weeks later that they'd put out a flyer on him, for murder, offering a reward of a hundred dollars. The man who had been Eric George Anthony, Sergeant of the 11th Ohio Cavalry, dropped from sight, and in his place appeared the nameless, taciturn drifter who was good with knife and gun and for hire – at a price – for anything. He drifted naturally into the orbit of Hercules Nix, and accepted the half-contemptuous sobriquet they gave him. Names were nothing. The Major believed only in staying alive, and he had managed to do so by never taking any chances. He'd learned that the best way of avoiding risk was by out-thinking, out-maneuvering, or out-gunning your opponent. He'd learned how at Bull Run and The Wilderness and Chickamauga, and again on the Powder River and the Bozeman Trail. He knew the best way to kill your enemy was from concealment, without warning, and ignoring such niceties as the 'even break.' He planned to go on living by these rules until he was old and rich, and that meant by definition that he was not about to go blundering into the jungly swamp after a proven mankiller the way Nix expected, the way the others were doing. They were dolts, anyway. Singlehandedly, Angel had out-witted them and killed half a dozen men mercilessly, yet still they blundered on. Fools! He had no intention of being another notch on Angel's tally-stick. He hung back, gradually letting the others get ahead of him. Moving in a criss-crossing fashion behind his comrades, stopping often, remaining motionless in dark and shadowed places, watching nothing, seeing everything, The Major was behind Angel when Angel moved out of hiding behind Watson and Mike Cheyney.

The Major's lips moved in what might have been a smile. He slithered carefully behind the equally careful Angel, unshipping from the scabbard at his side the twenty-inch bayonet which he had carried since the day he had been issued with it by the Army together with his breech-loading Springfield rifle. He had stolen it when they mustered him out, and worked lovingly on the weapon until it was a terrible killing tool. The long tapering blade was razor-edged on all the corners of its triangular upper section, its thin point honed to needle sharpness. Halfway up the blade, there were a series of serried notches sloping away from the point. When the blade was twisted inside a man and yanked out, it would gut him like a fish, as the tinhorn in Abilene had fatally discovered. Into the fitting normally filled by the rifle barrel, The Major had put a wooden haft that sat in his right hand snugly, securely. He held the bayonet with its needle point up in front of his body, about the level of a man's breastbone, and eeled silently in the wake of the broad-shouldered figure up ahead of him.

When Angel stopped, The Major made his move.

Angel had paused at the edge of a wide clearing perhaps ten yards across and five wide. He seemed to be checking carefully before stepping out into the open, poised to move forward. The Major saw that Angel's feet were apart, one ahead of the other, his weight on the forward foot and he struck, knowing that even if Angel heard him coming, it would take him a long second, maybe two, to redistribute his weight, turn, meet the assault. And in that long second, The Major would have killed him. The wicked bayonet point winked in a gray light as he drove it at Angel's back.

Angel had it timed to the millisecond.

He had heard the man behind him, placed him by sound, and wondered why he had not used a gun on him. Perhaps they had orders to take him alive, although that seemed unlikely in view of the events of the past day and a half. In which case, it had to be preference. The man behind him preferred to use some other weapon besides a gun: which meant a knife. So Angel took his chance, exposing his back and standing bad-footed, skin crawling against the expected smash of a treacherous bullet. You never heard the one that killed you, they said. Then he heard the sound, the rush of movement, the hiss of breath and he moved. Not as the man behind him would expect, turning to meet the attack, nor to one side or the other, which he might anticipate. Angel went straight forward into a somersault that would take him out of reach of the knife blade, and give him space to turn as the man adjusted and came at him again. He was up off the ground very fast, and ordinarily his ruse would have worked, but The Major was not an ordinary knife fighter, and what he had in his hand was not an ordinary knife. Even as he saw his first lunge miss and realized that Angel had partially outwitted him, The Major fell to the left and turned his forward movement into an upward slash to the right. An ordinary knife would not have even made contact, but The Major's bayonet was nearly two feet long, and the wicked point went through the outer edge of Angel's left triceps muscle, the long lifting muscle at the back of the upper arm. Like a rapier. As The Major pulled the weapon back, the serrated teeth ripped a long deep gash in the back of Angel's left arm, tearing a rasping shout of pain from his mouth as he rolled backward into the miry loam. Almost before he was on the ground, The Major was up and running at him, bayonet extended like a pitchfork aimed at Angel's belly. Angel rolled instinctively, and pain shot through his body as he lay on the wounded arm. His clothes were already spattered with blood. He swung a side kick that took The Major's kneecap apart and spilled him sprawling in the muck, his face smeared with it, partially blinding the man. Angel had a moment to get set as The Major pawed the mud from his eyes and came off the ground in a hobbling rush, and in that moment, Angel flicked his long-barreled Colt up out of the holster, earing back the hammer. He was very fast, but again he underestimated the long sweep of the bayonet. The Major's wide-armed swipe slammed the bayonet against the barrel of the Colt and jarred it out of Angel's mud-slimed grasp. In a lightning-fast movement, The Major whacked the bayonet back through the same arc in reverse. It made a soft noise – *whook!* – as Angel stumbled backward away from it, the blade missing his sucked-in belly by inches. The Major came after him, shambling on his good leg, slashing with the weapon as though it were a saber, *whook! whook! whook!* It was all Angel could do to get out of the way of the killing strokes, watching each movement of The Major's body for a slight change of posture, to be ready when the slash became a lunge. If the mud-smeared maniac pursuing him caught him in a sideways movement and changed that needlepoint slash into a lunge, Angel would be wide open. The Major's eyes were shiny with killing lust, and his breath rasped like a strangling snake. *Whook!* the bayonet went again, and Angel reeled back. *Whook! Whook!* Lunge. *Whook!*

It was only a matter of time before he made a mistake, and Angel didn't plan to wait until he made it. Avoiding the slashing cuts and thrusts had brought him around near a big rotting plantain tree, and he eased nearer to it. Many of the tree's arm-thick branches were dry and dead. Angel judged his distances: he wouldn't get two chances.

It was a macabre scene, the mud-smeared, limping figure with the killer's fixed grin and the glinting two-foot steel weapon pursuing the dodging, wearing quarry, never giving Angel a moment to rest, to counter-attack, trying constantly to get him backed up against one of the trees for the stopping stroke, somewhere The Major could cut him up a piece at a time.

The rain had stopped now, and steam rose from the panting bodies of the circling opponents. Their feet made juicy, sucking sounds in the trampled mud.

Whook! Whook, whook, whook, whook! The Major pursued his prey relentlessly, and still Angel managed to keep out of reach of the bayonet. Then, in one smooth sweep, he tore off one of the dead branches with his good right arm. The Major paused for a moment and then grinned when he saw what Angel seemed to be planning to use as a weapon. He slithered forward again, confident as ever as Angel broke the branch against the trunk of the tree, leaving himself with a three-foot length in his hand. Holding it in the classic dueling position, he moved forward at The Major, who gave a contemptuous laugh and smashed at the branch with his bayonet. A chunk of the rotted wood flew away into the under-growth, and splinters of the dried core gleamed whitely on the black mire for a moment before they were trampled underfoot. Now the broken branch was less than two feet long, and Angel's face registered dismay. The Major hissed with pleasure and smashed at the branch again, almost laughing at the expression of his opponent as another big chunk sailed into the air.

'Stupid bastard!' he shouted, and lunged in. To his astonishment, Angel did not dodge this time. Instead, he profiled his body, the way a matador does as the bull charges, letting the long bayonet pass him. As The Major was on the return step from his lunge, Angel turned back, pivoting in a tight half-circle. His right hand brought the short chunk of wood around his body and he jammed it onto the point of the bayonet as hard as he could. The Major pulled his weapon back, and then, with an almost impatient gesture, threw his arm wide to free it, tossing the speared chunk of wood away and turning back for the killing stroke, smiling like a weasel in a skylark's nest. It took one second, perhaps two, but it was enough for Angel.

His right hand had flickered down to the top of his mule-ear boot and it came up in a blur of movement. The Major's reflexes were very, very good. He even started to parry, as if knowing instinctively what was coming at him. However, reflex action is very rarely enough. The eye has to see and transmit, the brain receive and instruct, the arm hear and obey. It all happens in unmeasurable fractions of time, but still not fast enough to cancel out time elapsed. The slim silver Solingen blade thudded into The Major's throat just below his chin, shearing through windpipe, larynx, and gullet before neatly severing the spinal cord between the third and fourth vertebrae.

The Major's eyes bulged with disbelief, and he rose up on tiptoe, as though by doing so he could disengage the biting thing that had destroyed him. Then he collapsed like a dropped marionette, dead before he touched the earth.

Angel let out his breath in a long, long sigh.

It seemed as if he had been fighting for hours: every muscle in his body was alive with pain. He went across the clearing and picked up the fallen man's weapon. It was the knife of a thug, a barbarian; it disgusted him. He jammed the blade into a tree trunk and then put his full weight against it. The steel made a noise like a bullet hitting a bucket and then broke. He tossed the useless haft at The Major's deflated-looking body, realizing that he did not even know the name of the man he had killed.

'Take that to Hell with you!' he said venomously.

Now he ripped off the tattered sleeve of his shirt and looked at the ragged tear in his arm. The muscle was already numbing. When he tried to bend his arm he found he could not. He needed some time, a place where he could clean the wound, bandage it. Otherwise, he was at high risk. Gangrene from the filthy bayonet. Certain disability, fever. He had fought the Nix gang to a standstill, but The Major, although dead, had put a stop to that. He was in no shape to do any more fighting this day.

This in turn meant he had to move up the next part of his plan. There was nothing else open to him. He had to double back and head for the *hacienda*. It was a long way, but he could probably make it. Then a thought occurred to him that put a chill into his blood. Even if he made it, he was in pretty poor shape to take on the man he'd find there guarding Nix's lair: the Oriental, Yat Sen.

'Heads I lose, tails I lose,' he muttered. Then he got up and moved out.

FOURTEEN

Hercules Nix could take anything except defeat.

He had to confess, however, unwillingly, that so far Angel had out-thought him and out-fought his men every step of the way. He was no nearer taking the quarry now than he had been when they set out two days earlier from the *hacienda*. The stampede of the Indian ponies was a further example of Angel's resourcefulness, and his ambusher's war in the swamp had reduced the morale of Nix's men to nearly zero. They cared little or nothing for the death of their fellows, but they did care mightily for the manner of their own, and their guts were a-curdle from the sight of The Major's torn throat, the headless corpse of Bobbie Dirs, the transfixed skull of Rick Cross. This was not their way of fighting.

Nix had actually been in the Comanche encampment, negotiating for the labor of the Indian women and children with Koh-eet-senko's father-in-law, when Angel had stampeded the horses through the center of the village. Unlike the wily old savage with whom he was bargaining, Nix knew right away what had caused the breakout, and told Pah-hay-naka. 'Patches,' as the old man was known, had already informed him that Koh-eet-senko and the raiding warriors were due back within the next day, and now, as he pulled back to the edge of the swamp, his strength reduced by more than half, Hercules Nix smiled grimly in the dying light and vowed an awful vengeance.

He had not lost sight of the fact that it was he who was Angel's main target, he who Angel wished to bring down. He was conscious of an unease, not fear; and next morning, after a miserable night camped on the edge of the mosquito-riddled swamp, he led his remaining men toward the climbing dust cloud made by the returning war party.

They had come out of the north, turning at the end of the Comanche sickle trail that had brought them across the Rio Bravo and back to their own *querencia*. The dust of their passing glinted in the watery morning sunlight like a smokescreen against the yellow-dun hills, gullied and scarred like the faces of crones. Grotesque in their tinsel finery, Koh-eet-senko's raiding party came across the desert. Silvered bits on their horses, beads, scraps of colored cloth, glass or tin or fragments of mirror, gaudy bangles or bracelets bought from some passing *Comanchero* or ripped from the arm of a raped white woman, huge hooped earrings, their bodies painted for war, broad black stripes across face and forehead, their long straggling hair greased with bear fat or dressed with buffalo dung, they were dust-covered and ugly. The palpable stink of their presence was like the breath of the deepest pits of Hades.

The raid had been successful. Behind the war party trailed despondent Mexican women, some carrying children. They had been badly abused already, and knew that the worst was still to come. Many horses had been stolen, many guns, much plunder. There would be fat bellies in the camp tonight.

Hercules Nix did not ride straight up to the Comanche column. He knew better than to come at speed upon a raiding party. True, they knew him and knew that this valley was his, but they were still savages, without intelligence or understanding. A man could be killed just as dead by a trigger-happy Comanche buck who'd been sucking on a bottle of stolen liquor all the way home as by a trained assassin. Comanch' were like weather and women: entirely unpredictable. So Nix led his men slowly toward Koh-eet-senko's war party, riding alongside until the Indians recognized him. After a while, the Comanche leader made a lordly gesture: join us, it said. Nix nodded and kicked his stallion into a trot. The Comanches slowed down and made a big half-circle. They did not look particularly interested or uninterested. They were just there. They would see what was going to happen. Then, maybe, they would react. A palpable air of menace hung over them: cut-throats all, Nix thought. They looked indescribably evil. He had no misconceptions about them, but he needed them right now. He knew how to handle Koh-eet-senko. Subtlety, kindness, love, pity, all these were lost on the brute. He had risen in the ranks of the Comanch' because he was tougher, harder, bloodier, and more vicious than anyone else, a better thief, a better rider, a better hunter, and a better killer. It was inadvisable to make the mistake of forgetting these things when dealing with him.

Nix began his greeting with the usual fulsome compliments, superlatives, and lies.

Koh-eet-senko nodded, accepting them as no more than his due, looking around to make sure everyone else could hear what the white man was saying about him. Nix conducted his peroration in sign language: he could not speak the language of the Comanch' and he doubted anyone except another Comanch' could. It was like trying to wrap your tongue around a wriggling porcupine.

He waved an arm to include all his men, then with the index finger and middle finger of his right hand, he made a zigzag pattern in front of his eyes, after which he extended his hand forward. 'We are hunting,' these signs said. Then he made the signs for a white man: the right index finger drawn across the forehead to indicate a sombrero. 'We are hunting a white man.'

Koh-eet-senko nodded and swatted at the flies buzzing around the bloody scalps on his horse's mane. He was impatient to get back to the camp, to his women. They had been on the war trail a long time.

Nix now held his hand over his head in the sign for a tall man, then rubbed the tips of the fingers of his right hand on the back of the left, following these signs with the sign for shelling corn. 'A tall man,' he was saying, 'with hair the color of corn.' Nix placed his palms parallel, facing each other, taking the right hand back a little and moving it up and down. He turned his left palm up to the sky and placed his right forefinger on it. Then, with his right palm facing upward, slightly bent, he pushed his right hand forward. 'Help us,' he had said. 'And I will give you–' He waited, making sure that he had Koh-eet-senko's attention. He had. The Comanche had become alert at the sign for 'give' and his eyes glowed with greed as Nix made the sign for a rifle, left hand holding the imaginary barrel, right forefinger cocked on the trigger, and added 'many, many.'

There was a murmur of interest from the other Comanches. Guns was a subject that interested them all. More guns equalled more plunder. Koh-eet-senko turned his back on Nix and spoke rapidly in Comanche to two other Indians as virulently ugly as himself. They seemed to be arguing vehemently, but their colloquy lasted only a few minutes. Then Koh-eet-senko folded his arms, faced Nix, and nodded.

Nix pasted a smile on his face and extended his hand. The Comanche looked at it for a moment as if it were a snake, and then his brow cleared and with a gap-toothed smile he pumped away at Nix's hand as if life itself depended on the handshake. Then Koh-eet-senko extended his left hand, and with the right forefinger, pulled aside the left forefinger and pointed at the middle one: the sign for 'tomorrow.'

Nix shook his head violently. No, he signalled, making another sign. He held his right index finger in front of his face, pushed it forward quickly a couple of inches, then brought it back. He repeated the signal. 'Now, now.'

Koh-eet-senko made an angry sound and spat out a series of Gatlin-gun gutturals. Even without Comanche, Nix knew damned well what they meant, and he held up his hand palm out, in the peace sign.

'Very well,' he said, nodding, smiling, placating the Indian. 'Tomorrow.' He made the sign for daybreak and Koh-eet-senko nodded curtly, not knowing how Nix was cursing him: Jesus Christ alone knew what Angel could get up to in a whole day. He realized Koh-eet-senko was telling him something, crossing the index finger of both hands and then making the hand-to-mouth signs for eating. These he followed by placing his palms parallel opposite each other and moving them up and down and away from each other and back. 'Come camp eat dance' was what the signs said, but Nix knew what they meant. Koh-eet-senko and his warriors were going to celebrate their successful raid. They were going to eat themselves sick, drink themselves stupid, then roll into the blankets with their verminous squaws. They would be even more slow-witted and surly than usual at daybreak, and many of them would refuse to join the band which would accompany Nix in pursuit of the white man. That was their privilege, and there wasn't a damned thing Koh-eet-senko or anyone else could do about it. Nix stifled his anger. There wasn't a damned thing he could do about Koh-eet-senko's invitation, either. To refuse his hospitality would be to court disaster; he was more than aware of the difference in the strength of Koh-eet-senko's band and his own, and he knew the Indian was, too.

'Good,' he wig-wagged. 'We are coming.'

Once again Koh-eet-senko nodded, as though he had known all along that no other response was possible. He kicked his painted pony into a walk and the warriors fell into line behind him.

'Hey, boss,' Des Elliott whispered urgently as Nix followed suit. 'Where we headin'?'

'We're going to a party,' Nix said sourly. 'So look as if you like the idea. Tell the men to keep their guns handy and stay close together. And that means until we ride out of that camp, got it?'

'You bet I got it,' Elliott said. 'You know what?'

'What?'

'I ain't sure I wouldn't have rather stayed in the swamp with Angel.'

Angel was long gone from the swampy lakeside.

The late afternoon sun was hot, and welcome after the steamy-dank atmosphere of the jungly undergrowth. It took away the persistent chill sourness from Angel's body as he made his way south along the river, but he wasn't in good shape and he knew it. His wounded arm throbbed, and his head was light. He felt sometimes as if he was having to reach his feet down to touch the ground, a strange, floaty feeling that came and went. Once he found himself lying face down in the dirt with no clear recollection of how he had gotten there. He didn't see the dustcloud raised by the returning *Hoh'ees* tribe, nor the smaller one raised by Nix and his men as they arrowed across to intercept Koh-eet-senko's warriors. Frank Angel was too intent on just making the next bend in the river, using cover and watching for pursuit. Most of all he was intent on just plain keeping going: it was a long way to the *hacienda* and his troubles would be far from over when he got there. Nightfall found him about halfway to his destination, and he stopped to rest because he had to. He decided he would risk a tiny belly-fire, the kind hunting Apaches build when they are on the killing trail, a tiny fire burning in a deep-scooped hole over which the warrior arches his body, concealing the faint glow and receiving body warmth to keep out the deep chill of the desert night.

He took out the flat silver flask that had been included in his survival kit, and splashed some of the brandy on his ragged arm wound. It stung like liquid fire as he mopped the wound clean with strips torn from his shirt. He took a healthy swig of the spirit, feeling it course through his body, a moving glow that settled in his empty belly. With a regretful shrug he poured the rest out on the ground. He needed the flask more than the liquor, and with great care he filled the flask with water from the shallowest edge of the river. Then he put it on the glowing coals of his tiny fire and when it was boiled, used it to clean and disinfect the arm wound. It was stiffened and swollen, but the firm dressing of shirt-cloth and the cleansing effect of the water and the brandy eased the pain. His arm pulsed now as if alive, but he was at least reasonably confident that there was no infection in the wound. When that was done, he fed some more of the tiny dry sticks into his fire hole, then wormed into the undergrowth and sat, as unmoving as a stone idol, while the night strengthened its hold over the starstrewn sky, and the creatures of the night grew bold and left their lairs.

The big old jackrabbit never had a chance. He lolloped into Angel's range, nostrils twitching, ready to hitch-kick his way out of danger at the slightest movement. But he was downwind of the stone-still man who sat with the slim Solingen steel throwing knife laid against his right shoulder. The jack hopped nearer, foraging, and then erupted into movement as it saw the whip-down movement of Angel's hand, but fast as it was, the knife was faster.

'Supper in the pot,' Angel said, and started skinning the rabbit. He gutted and cleaned it where it had fallen. Owls and other night predators would clean up after him, and leave no waste. Nature's food cycle was beautifully worked out. He carried the carcass back to his little fire, and now cut a long thin stick from which he stripped the bark. Then two Y-shaped branches were jammed into the ground, the rabbit spitted with the longer one.

When he had finished eating, Angel made a brush mattress and lay back to rest for a little while. He knew he would get no sleep this night, and he would need to muster as much strength as he could beforehand. He lay completely relaxed, letting his toes slacken, then his ankles, then the calves, the knees, all the way up his body. He put all thought out of his head and concentrated upon the figure one. He held the image of it in the front of his mind, and when any other thought intruded he shoved it back away, returning to the figure one. After a little while his breathing slowed, his heartbeat deepened. He remained like this for perhaps half an hour, or a little longer. Then he got himself ready to move on.

It was full dark now, and the stars were sprinkled all over the sky. Someone had once told him that on a night like this you could see up to two thousand five hundred of them. There seemed to be more, somehow, and close enough to reach up and touch. A soft breeze had sprung up from the south, and the soft purr of the river made a gentle background to his thoughts. He might have been alone in the world, moving undiscovered through some garden wilderness. He smiled at his thoughts. This valley might be many things, but it was not a garden. Now he saw the lights of the *hacienda* ahead of him in the darkness, and he moved more cautiously, wary as any fox. He had one vital task to perform before he went inside the stockade, and he moved up the riverside to the place where it must be done. Then he stood erect and drew in a deep, deep breath. It was time. Now, somehow, he had to go in there and kill the deadly Oriental, Yat Sen.

Or get killed trying.

FIFTEEN

He waited until the hours before dawn.

He was conscious of wasted time, but it was time he had to waste. He needed all the advantage he could get, and even one as small as this. Yat Sen was not an ordinary man, but man he was, and like all men, his reflexes and his resistance would be at their lowest in the cold hours before the false dawn. With the handicap of his wounded arm, Angel needed all the advantage he could manage, and on this basis he picked his time. He knew, as all doctors know, as all tyrants and secret police have always known, that it is in the deathwatch hours that fear grows to the size of a monster. The doctors know they will lose their weak ones, the ones already near death, in these empty, unfriendly hours. The tyrants know that it is the time to come and hammer on the door and shout your name. The secret police know it is in the hours before dawn that you will finally break. The stockade was silent when he went over the wall, dark and deserted. There were no guards. Angel worked his way around the deep-shadowed wall, getting his bearings again, seeing some things he had not seen the first time.

In the northeastern corner of the stockade was a long earthen ramp and squatting at its flattened crest, muzzle poking out and aimed more or less at the site of the Comanche encampment, was a well-kept Army cannon, a twelve-pounder by the look of it. There was a pyramid of shells at one side of it, a powder bucket suspended from the center of the axle. Angel allowed himself a thin smile: Nix had not been jesting when he said he used the Comanches but did not trust them.

He flitted like a ghost across the open space to the lower arm of the L-shaped *hacienda*. In this short extension to the main house was housed the machinery that supported Hercules Nix's domain, the pumps and the switches and the controls that sent water down the valley, filled the lake beside the Indian camp, kept the swampy jungle and the muddy lake alive. He thought back to Welsh Al Davies and the fetid fleabag hotel in Galveston. It seemed like years ago.

Like an extension of one of the shadows that sheltered him, Angel moved to the door of the machine room. It was, like all the doors in the building, of solid oak lined with steel. He bent close to examine the locks. Double-action tumbler locks by the look of them. Far too good to be picked, even by a trained man like himself, without tools. In books, people opened doors with little lengths of metal, or a lady's hairpin. In real life it was a little harder. A man named Joseph Bramah had once patented a lock that took an experienced locksmith over fifty-one hours to pick. That was using all the right tools, and more than ninety years ago. There was a man back East named Linus Yale who had acted as instructor to the Justice Department. He had shown them the secrets of every kind of lock, and designed lockpicks for them to open them with. Yet even he had admitted that many locks would simply take too damned long to open, and that the surest way to get into a building quickly was to blow the damned door down. Well, he couldn't do that. Not just yet, anyway.

First, there was the matter of Yat Sen.

In the cool-shadowed darkness, he slowly stripped off his clothes, leaving only a makeshift loincloth made from the remnants of his shirt. He padded softly around the house to the patio in front of the building, and stood there, mustering himself. When his breathing was deep and controlled, he knew he was as ready as he'd ever be.

'Yat Sen!' he shouted. 'Yat Sen!'

He was about to shout again when a light went on upstairs, then another. He waited, poised on the cold stone floor, the chill breeze raising gooseflesh on his naked body. Light glinted on the knife in his hand. He wanted Yat Sen to see the knife. The curtains of one of the second-story rooms twitched, and he thought he could see the slim shape of Victoria Nix, her eyes dark smudges in the pale blur of her face.

Then Yat Sen loomed in the doorway, his squat body silhouetted against the lighted interior. There was no expression on his face. He looked at Angel and then at the knife in Angel's hand and nodded.

'Boss say you plob'ly pletty good. Him dead?'

'Not yet, Yat Sen,' Angel said. 'He's got to be broken before I kill him.'

'Ah,' Yat Sen said, nodding again. 'Un'stan' this.'

'I have to help the woman, Yat Sen,' Angel said, watching the Oriental like a hawk for any sudden movement. 'Are you going to try to stop me?'

'Yes,' Yat Sen said, as if he had been deliberating. 'But un'stan' this also.'

'Well,' Angel said, crouching slightly. 'Get at it.'

Yat Sen came forward, hands weaving, body crouched and tense, legs bent slightly, and the slit eyes almost closed in concentration. He had on only a pair of cotton drawers, and his solid, hard body gleamed like old oiled brass. Then without warning his body arched into a running kick so fast that Angel almost failed to respond. He recovered on the instant and slashed the knife up and across in a whipping arc designed to slit the tendon of one of Yat Sen's flying heels. Yet he missed, for somehow the Oriental did something Angel had never seen any man do. He modified his flying kick, turning his body and pulling back one foot that rapped hard against the inside of Angel's forearm, jarring his slash off target. Then Yat Sen had landed in a crouch and was moving again before he stopped turning, a hiss emerging from his compressed mouth as his right hand flickered forward like a striking snake. Angel struck down at it with the knife and as he moved knew he had been fooled. Yat Sen's feint left his right side exposed, and he just managed to parry a scything blow that would have broken his neck by blocking Yat Sen's rock-hard forearm with his own left arm. The brutal shock of the collision brought a yell of pain from Angel, and he rolled back and away from Yat Sen before the Oriental could strike again. Up on his feet in an instant, he thought he saw a flare of realization in Yat Sen's narrowed eyes and cursed the luck. Now Yat Sen would know he was hurt, and he would follow up, punishing him by striking repeatedly at the weak spot. Yat Sen was fighting in the *Tai-Chi Chuan* fashion, but he had discarded that discipline's soft and graceful movements for a brutal, killing style. Angel came up out of his crouch and tried again with the knife, but fast as he was, Yat Sen was even faster. His foot slammed into Angel's wrist, numbing the hand, and simultaneously the Oriental whipped his right hand upward and across, smashing it against the upper part of Angel's left arm. The knife looped upward, catching a flicker of light from the windows, and disappeared soundlessly into the bushes as Angel felt the warm gush of blood under his wounded arm. He backed away, guard up, and Yat Sen stalked after him, the wicked trace of a smile on his slash of a mouth. He came in fast and struck, one-two, one, one-two, then retreated as quickly. Although Angel struck the man very hard several times with his good right hand, he might as well have been hitting a plank for all the effect it seemed to have on Yat Sen. Yat Sen grinned and came in again, and hit Angel beneath the ribcage with a looping chop that completely defeated Angel's attempt to parry it. The blow whacked the breath out of the American's body, and he was stock still for a moment in which Yat Sen hit him hard across the bony protuberance above the right ear. Angel went down on the stone patio with bells ringing in his head and a roaring blackness behind his eyes. Through the mist he saw the squat figure coming at him, and he kicked out upward in sheer desperation, catching Yat Sen's kneecap and spilling him in a rolling ball. Yat Sen was up and ready for the counter-attack that Angel had been unable to launch, and grinned for real, now. Cat and mouse, Angel thought, as the breath labored back into his lungs. He realized Yat Sen was pulling his blows, playing with him to make the combat take a little longer. The moon face was beaming with the confident knowledge of being able to end the contest whenever Yat Sen wished to do so, and Angel felt a faint, distant feather-touch of fear. The man was impervious to hurt. He had hit him a dozen times with blows that would have stopped any ordinary man in his tracks, dead. They just glanced off the coppery hide.

Yat Sen came in again with his bullet head down, but this time Angel knew it was a feint, The Oriental would never expose his neck like that. He took two rapid steps to the side, his knee moving in a strike as much artifice as was Yat Sen's, and like a flash the Oriental threw himself to the side, tense ball of right foot moving upward at Angel's groin in a kick that would have put Angel down, retching like a dog, had it landed. But Angel's movement was a feint, and Yat Sen was momentarily committed. As Yat Sen lay back and kicked upward, Angel changed his own movement like lightning, and his own right foot came around in a wicked arc. His clenched foot smashed viciously into Yat Sen's throat and hurled him away, to land hunched over and coughing to get air into his paralyzed windpipe. Now Angel went after him like a striking kestrel, and again his foot moved in that tight, vicious arc. The force of the impact on Yat Sen's back numbed the trained foot, and Yat Sen's body lurched over in a rictus of agony as the enormous shock of the kick burst soft organs inside him. He rolled on his back and struck at Angel's legs with a forearm like a block of mahogany, and Angel went down on one knee, but as he did, he again struck at Yat Sen's throat with his hand. Yat Sen's bullet head bounced on the stone patio, but he was already starting to get up. Before he could make it, Angel went high over Yat Sen's body and came down, right heel rigid, stamping with all his weight and strength on the man's exposed belly. Yat Sen contorted like some obscene rubber doll, and for the first time a moan of agony escaped his clenched lips, followed by an awful gout of thick black slime. Mercilessly, Angel followed up his advantage, turning his body to strike again at the defenseless throat but somehow, suffering agonies that would have long since destroyed another man, Yat Sen parried his blow and rolled to his feet. He was lurching, and his eyes were wild with pain, but he was up, and Angel watched in disbelief as the terrible bleeding thing came at him. Yat Sen was as good as dead and both of them knew it. Imbued with the death-insanity of the Orient, he intended somehow to take his opponent with him. Angel could not hurt him any more: so he came at his enemy like some wounded ape, the front of his body streaked with internal blood and the other awful slime. His weaving arms reached for Angel, who struck them down and moved away. Still Yat Sen came on, and Angel knew he must kill the pursuing thing or it would kill him. He scooped up a heavy oak stool that lay on its side beneath a bush at the side of the patio, and let Yat Sen get nearer. When he was near enough, he hit the Oriental with the stool. It was a solid, heavy blow, and not even Yat Sen could parry it. It smashed in the side of his skull and he went down on his knees, screeching as lancing lines of light burst through his broken brain. While he was down on his knees, Angel hit him again. Yat Sen somehow reacted, the oak-solid right arm raised to parry the blow, and this time the stool splintered as it struck. The stool was a ruin, but so was Yat Sen's arm. It flapped down, bone protruding from the battered flesh.

Yat Sen looked up at his conqueror with eyes that were drowning in the acid of death, then astonishingly, from what source Angel could not even imagine, the light and sapience came back into them. Yat Sen came up off his knees much, much faster than anyone as badly hurt as he could have done by any human measurement. But Yat Sen's strength was superhuman, fanatic, and he beat aside Angel's blows and clamped his good left hand on Angel's throat. The two men went down with a crash that seemed to shake the house, and Angel felt the hot sticky pulse of Yat Sen's blood on his own naked body. With his own good right hand, he used what was left of the stool to hammer at Yat Sen's elbow, but the man's arm was too close, and the power was gone from Angel's arms. Yat Sen was an unbudgeable weight, and his fetid breath burned raggedly on Angel's face as Angel eeled and humped his body to try to get out from beneath Yat Sen. Yat Sen sensed the movements, and like some dying anaconda, wrapped his mighty legs around Angel's, the muscle bulging at the desperate urging of his broken brain, nothing left alive in the whole broken frame except the will, the determination to take the thing that had killed it down to hell when it went.

Angel felt his own breathing go ragged,

and the clawing fingers tightened spasmodically on his windpipe, relentlessly cutting off the air. There were dark edges on his vision, and red rockets exploded behind his eyes. He beat repeatedly at the clutching hand, the battered arm, but to no avail and steadily more weakly. Darkness was coming up out of the ground and beginning to swallow him.

He knew he had only seconds left.

There is a place in the mind which you can train, a place from which, at the extreme moment of peril, you can summon a special strength. Kee Lai, the little Korean instructor who had first told him of *Sh'oo Lin* and *Tai-Chi Chuan*, *Ninjitsu* and *Bando*, the method Angel used to fight, called this strength *ch'i*. There was no Occidental word for it. It was something of the mind itself, of the spirit and the body combined that on summons becomes all of the self in one moment at one place. Angel stopped struggling for just the moment he needed, and the sudden slackness of his body communicated itself into the red flower of Yat Sen's pain. Yat Sen's killing grip lessened for an instant, and in that immeasurable moment, Angel summoned all of himself and moved.

He surged upright, lifting the dead weight

of Yat Sen as if the Oriental were a clinging child. His hands moved, irresistible. They broke Yat Sen's grip and he staggered back on his heels. As he did, Angel hit him with a brutal angled hand chop on the left side of the neck. There is medical terminology for the effect of such a blow, names for the things that break beneath its force. But no one has ever charted the actual moment of impact: for no one has ever survived it. Yat Sen went down on his knees like a traitor awaiting the executioner's ax. Yet still he would not die, still a faint spark flickered in the red madness of his broken brain. Somehow, he found enough strength to raise his head, to grunt something that at first Angel could not fathom.

'Ugg. Ann,' Yat Sen Croaked. 'Egg ugg ann.'

Good man, he was saying. Very good man. It was unbelievable, and Angel stood there unbelieving as the thing on the floor got up. Angel's hands hung limp at his sides. He had nothing left at all and still Yat Sen was coming at him, like something out of a nightmare, the broken body still trying to find and destroy the enemy that had killed it. Yat Sen lurched forward another step, leaving a bloody footprint where he had trodden, then another. Angel watched, hypnotized, rabbit before cobra. Yat Sen took one more step and then, behind him, Victoria Nix pulled both triggers of the shotgun. It went off with a sound like the ultimate end of the world. The barrels were so close to Yat Sen's back that the unspread charge almost cut him in two. He was whammed off his feet as if he had been roped by a man on a galloping horse, and went past Angel bowed outward, his belly a burst mass of torn tissue.

The body toppled into the water of the pool with an enormous flat splash that threw water six feet high. Then, after just a moment, the surface began to churn. Victoria Nix looked at the place where Yat Sen's body had sunk in a cloud of spreading pink. The shaft of light from the house revealed a writhing, shimmering mass of silver.

Angel didn't bother to look. He took her hand and turned her away from the bright, shuddering, shifting movement in the water. Maybe she didn't know what it was, but he did.

SIXTEEN

The genus is called *Characin*.

Squat, spiny, ugly little fish. They have terrifying jaws full of tiny barbed teeth and they are without question one of Nature's most merciless creations. Not many people know them by their real name, but they are more often than not called piranha.

Angel had discovered their presence in Hercules Nix's man-made river very quickly. He had stopped on his first day to fill his waterskin and the terrible little fish had surged up out of the roiled water as if drawn to his hand by magnets, sending him floundering back out of the shallows in shameless haste. After that, he had used extreme care to take water, dipping in only the clearest, shallowest eddies of the stream. Those dreadful little creatures could take the flesh off a cavalry horse inside an hour and their presence in the river had made him wonder yet again at the mind of the man who had put them there. He wondered how many men had unwittingly waded into the water, relishing its cool touch, until suddenly the myriad slashing rips of the greedy teeth had spilled their blood into the uncaring water, there to bring even larger hordes of the greedy fish. Below the *hacienda*, Angel had come across a wire-meshed gate that spanned the river. It was pretty much the same kind of contraption that they used in fish farms, constructed from steel and wood and wire mesh, an effective barrier to the little beasts getting inside the enclave. On the bank of the river there had been a small capstan and a metal rod to turn it, and without compunction Angel had winched up the gate so that by now the fish would have found free access to all of Hercules Nix's waterways. It was Angel's hope that they would in due course find their way through the system and emerge in the lake alongside the Comanche camp. It appealed to the macabre side of his sense of humor to visualize the first Comanch' who took a swim in the lake after the fish found their way there.

Now he put his arm around Victoria Nix's trembling shoulders and led her away from the awful sight of the bubbling feast in the formerly silent pool. A great weariness was coming down on Angel, and as the adrenalin drained from his nervous system, it seemed as if someone was replacing it with molten lead. Every bone in his body seemed to be squeaking with deadly fatigue, and the ripped wound beneath his arm was throbbing like a child banging a drum. He shook his head to clear it, wondering what would have happened if Victoria Nix had not appeared on the patio.

Actually, the answer was inescapably simple: Yat Sen would have killed him. He recalled his earlier decision to use the deathwatch hours to catch Yat Sen at a low ebb. If that had been the Oriental's low ebb, it was a damned good job he didn't try him at high noon. It seemed like a good joke, and he was smiling fatly at it as he slid into a sitting position on the floor of the hall-way into the house. Victoria Nix made a surprised, concerned sound and crouched beside him, trying to lift him up.

'Try to stand,' she said, putting her arms around him. 'I'll help you.'

He was greasy with sweat and blood, and far away in his mind the thought formed that it was pretty unchivalrous of him to get this lovely woman in her long, soft nightdress all smeared up with blood and sweat and the other mess of combat.

'Now,' she said, panting as she tried to

move him. 'Come on.'

'On,' he said, and somehow got to his feet. He heard her grunt with exertion and realized that he was putting most of his weight on her. She was a lot stronger than she looked, he thought. Most women were, he thought then. He wondered why he was covered in sweat. Her voice sounded as if it was coming down a long, long tunnel.

Little men inside his head were using steel drills to get out, timing each twist to the throb of his heart. He gagged as Victoria Nix poured brandy down his throat, but the liquid fire that blazed in its wake stifled the throbbing pain. He decided to sit down and he was unconscious before his back hit the seat rest of the chair.

She let him sleep an hour, knowing it was all they could spare.

He awoke to find her holding a tray carrying a bowl of soup, some bread, a glass of milk. His mind was fogged, but his body felt stronger and he realized that she had dressed his wound, and that his body was clean. She must have washed him, covered him with the soft blanket.

'Well,' she said. 'Can you eat something?'

She was dressed in a white man-style shirt

and a divided riding skirt, and she looked efficient. He wondered whether she had chosen the mannish clothes deliberately, or whether her subconscious had been at work. She looked like a nurse, and her appearance removed for both of them any sense of embarrassment.

'How long was I unconscious?' he said, swinging his legs to the floor. His head felt a little light, but it was something he could live with. He told her to put the food on the table.

'Out near the main gate, behind some bushes, you'll find my clothes,' he said. 'Would you go and get them for me? And while you're at it, find the keys to every lock in the place. Can you do that?'

She nodded, her eyes large with the question she wanted to ask him. He knew what it was and he shook his head.

'No, Victoria,' he said. 'Nix isn't dead. Come daylight, he'll be out there looking for me again. It won't take him long to narrow it down to here.'

'I thought,' she said. 'I hoped – when you came back last night. I – watched. I thought, he's come back. You were the first one that ever came back.'

'The others never had the chance to,

Victoria,' he said softly. 'Nix killed them all. He hunted them down like animals and killed them. He's trying to do the same thing to me.'

She frowned as if the concept were beyond her imagination. 'All of them?' she said wonderingly. She didn't need his confirming nod, and the shock went out of her eyes to be replaced with slow realization. She was putting memories together, seeing them in a new context.

'Then he is a murderer, too,' she breathed. 'A murderer, too.'

'He always was,' Angel said. 'You must have known.'

'No,' she said softly. 'He – he was just *there*. I never asked. Couldn't ask. I wasn't me. I was some kind of thing. Something he used.'

'Tell me,' he said softly, knowing she had to get it out of her or it would break her completely.

'I can't,' she began. There was a long moment's silence, and then she began to cry, quite soundlessly, huge tears welling from her eyes and falling with audible plops to the floor. Angel wanted to go to her, put his arms around her and hold her until the trembling stopped, but he knew better.

After perhaps two minutes, she looked at him, and tried for a brave little smile. 'I can't explain it, you'd never understand,' she faltered.

'Try me.'

'It was just... I'd never experienced anything. Living with Daddy, I never – oh, there were boys, of course. But nothing – like him. He was – brutal. I – tried. He would laugh at me. Tell me what would happen to Daddy if I wasn't nice. Nice! Do you know what he meant by nice? There was no one I could tell. I couldn't tell Daddy what he was doing to me. Somehow, I didn't have the courage to tell anyone else. I felt so alone, so alone. And he was always there, always there. After a while I began to forget that there had ever been a time when he was not there. He was my present and my future, and he obliterated my past. I didn't think of him the way I thought of any other man I knew. He was something bigger, blacker, stronger. A force I could not – contest. I tried at first. But he was more cruel if I tried to fight, and in the end I just stopped. Stopped fighting, resisting, anything. I accepted, and he took me. And more and more and more of me. Until there was nothing left. Somehow it had become the most important thing in my life to cook the food he liked, to wear the clothes he liked, to do – what pleased him. If he was pleased with me, he was not cruel, he was even kind to Daddy. Daddy was sick then. If I didn't do – some of the things he wanted me to do, he took it out on Daddy. So I obeyed. I became dependent on him, alert to his moods, watching his eyes to anticipate his desires. His thing. His tame, willing thing. No use for anything else.'

Her self-loathing was cold and empty, her need naked and childlike. He went to her now, put his arm around her, drew her close to him and patted her gently, soothing her like a child awakened by thunder.

'You saved my life,' he said. 'I never thanked you for that.'

'That man!' she said her voice muffled against his chest. 'I hated him. I hated him.' Her shudders lessened, and he held her until he felt her tears drying, her trembling stop. Her breathing became softer, deeper, and he sensed small shiftings of her body against his own, the delicate signals of woman to man. He took both her shoulders in his hands and held her away at arm's length. Her eyes were luminous, deep and mysterious and far-away-looking.

'Go get my clothes, Victoria,' he told her, and she nodded without speaking, deer-shy. She ran lightfootedly out of the room and as she went Angel damped down a curse of discontent. There were no corners in his timetable for romantic interludes, and a dependent woman was a ball and chain if a man was fighting for his life. Yet after what she had told him, he knew he couldn't abandon her, although she had been no part of his plan until the moment she pulled the triggers of the shotgun behind Yat Sen. He thought about Hercules Nix, and what was left of his killer band. He thought of their possible movements, their probable intentions. By the time Victoria came back with his clothes bundled in front of her, Angel had decided how to fight Hercules Nix. Then he set about getting ready to do it.

SEVENTEEN

In war, as in love, timing is all.

If, along with timing, you are gifted with luck by the gods, then the odds are in your favor. Equally, luck withheld alters the odds against you. This day, for the first time, Hercules Nix felt that his timing was bad, his luck running sour, and experienced the first faint tendril touches of apprehension. Prior to this day he had set such doubts scornfully aside but now, as he led his men out of the Comanche village, he could do so no longer. In spite of his promises, bribes, cajolings, in spite of the assurances given by Koh-eet-senko, the Comanches did not want to go hunting the fugitive white man. They wanted the squalid comfort of their teepees, the agile giggling embraces of their women, and nothing Nix could say or do would alter their decision. Comanches, like all Indians, hunted and fought only when the mood was upon them. They might ride several hundred miles with a raiding party, only to back away from the skirmish line without warning or explanation, and turn their pony's head for home. No Indian considered such an action either shameful or cowardly, although many white men found it inexplicable. Indians understood that a man might suddenly realize his medicine was bad, his luck soured, his timing off. No tribal law decreed that he should stand and fight and maybe die if his intuition, his guiding spirit, or some omen he had spotted told him not to. This day, with their bellies full of rotgut, bodies sated with sex and food and boasting, teepees crawling with admiring squaws rummaging with excited jabber through the plunder, there were few of Koh-eet-senko's warriors willing to climb aboard their ponies and slog about the valley, no matter what the reward. After all, brother, a man can only carry one rifle and one lance into battle. A man can only bed one woman at a time. A man can only eat and drink his fill, live in one teepee at a time. Why go to the trouble of catching up one's horse, riding out into the hard flat heat of the day, to do the white man's work for him? The whole tribe of *Hoh'ees*, all the Timber People to catch one fugitive white man? Come, brother, there are the village girls, the tangy taste of young puppy stew, the black bottles of firewater, and many stories to tell. We'll hunt and fight some other day.

So Nix rode out of the village with a smaller force of warriors than he had bargained for. Koh-eet-senko had kept his own promise, albeit with much grumbling and demands for more booty. The Comanches were in vacation mood, laughing and boasting about their sexual prowess the preceding night.

It took all of Nix's iron control not to lash out at them, but he knew that to do so would simply result in their turning back and abandoning him. Right now he needed them, so he bided his time and bit his tongue. He fed Koh-eet-senko compliments until his own gorge rose, and after about an hour of it, Koh-eet-senko dispatched an arrowhead of four warriors to check along the bank of the river. The larger remnant he led back to the swamp. The Comanches would check it out in no time: their tracking skills would lay bare Angel's tracks as if he had painted them red. Comanche seek, Comanche find: there is no escape from the hunters of the *Nermernuh*, Koh-eet-senko declaimed grandly.

Withal, Nix still felt uneasy, out of tune with his own confidence. He stifled his anger as the Comanches raced their horses around, showing off in front of the stone-faced white men, performing all sorts of incredible feats of horsemanship, whooping and shouting and managing their animals with splendid but pointless skill. The fact that they were raising more dust than a herd of buffalo seemed not to matter to them, and when Nix remonstrated with Koh-eet-senko, the Comanche leader raised surprised eyebrows. Was

Nix frightened that one man would see them? What could that one man do, where could he run in the country of the Comanche? Again Nix swallowed his anger, cursing his bad luck and his bad timing, determined that in spite of them he would win anyway. The gods smiled at that.

Nix's bad luck was Angel's good fortune. His timing was made perfect by the period of grace Nix's dealings with the Comanche gave him, and he used it to formidable effect. If good fortune it was, then good fortune sent a soft soughing breeze into the valley from the southwest that stirred the drooping trees beside Nix's deadly pool, and lifted small spirals of dust that ran across the open ground like dying ghosts. His strength waxing as the rest and the food restored it, Angel spent vital hours in the room full of machinery behind the *hacienda*, familiarizing himself with the functions, workings, and connections of the machines before he began to make his alterations. Once he knew the inter-relationship between machine and pump and huge, clumsy leaden battery, he set diligently to work rephasing, rewiring, rearranging. His plan had to be simple, for he did not know how much time he had. It also had to be effective. Which meant it had to be brutal. When he was done, he told Victoria to change her clothes and she worked alongside him with shovel and crowbar until her soft hands were raw and bleeding, until Angel felt that someone had been working on the base of his spine with an ax.

Every half hour or so, he stopped her and sent her to the watchtower to scan the open land to the north for any sign of movement, a dust cloud, anything. His purpose was twofold; to give her respite from the backbreaking labor, and to ensure that Nix did not run them down while they were out in the open. There was some desperation in the way he worked, for he did not know whether he could complete what he had to do, but by the time the sun started its long slide down the western sky, the outdoor work was done and there was still no sign of Hercules Nix and his men. Now the two of them moved into the welcome shade of the stockade to finish what needed finishing there. They were close to the end of that when Victoria saw the spiral of dust to the north.

The hunters were coming.

Now Angel took a five-gallon can of kerosene and ran with it across the open land, about a quarter of a mile angling southeast to where the first low spur of the foothills marked the effective end of the scrubland and sparse, dry grass. He gauged his own position carefully in relationship to the smudge of dots beneath the dust on the horizon, and the wide-thrown gates of the stockade. The wind was not strong, but it was more than strong enough. He ran back now, splashing the coal oil in a wide swathe around him, on greasewood and sage-brush and brittle, brown grass. Then, when he was back at the stockade gate, he fired the grass. A low blue flame ran flickering away from his feet, turning to a noise like the sudden exhalation of a gutshot horse, and all at once the scrubland was on fire. An oily black cloud of smoke rose angled to the sky, and the prairie grass and bushes curled, smoked, sparked, and roared into yellow flame that reached along the ground toward the north, greedy for more, fed by the steady breeze. Now the smoke coiled in huge eddies toward the brassy sky, and the fire advanced in a long line that stretched from the rocky wall of the mountains on the southern edge of the valley to the reed-shadowed edges of the manmade river. It sucked oxygen from the air and fed greedily on it, making a huge, irresistible marching wall of flame and smoke. Even behind the thick wall of logs, the heat was unbearable, and Angel pulled Victoria back into the stockade, past the twelve pounder which he had manhandled into a new position, and up on the ramp it had formerly occupied. From there, through the shifting screen of smoke and the rising, eddying blur of the heat waves from the fire, he could see the hunters reacting to the oncoming fire. It was not moving very fast, perhaps no more than the speed of a running man. But it was inexorable, total, unstoppable.

Ahead of the seeking tongues of fire ran myriad small creatures: jackrabbit and kangaroo rat, desert fox and skunk, quail and rattlesnake and owl, fleeing for survival.

Angel watched the fire without expression.

If it kept on its present course, it would march right up to the edge of the wood in which the Comanche encampment was pitched. It would probably fire the trees: they would be as dry as tinder at this time of year. It would certainly drive the Comanches out of their camp, and it might well be that it would kill women, children, and old people as it did. So be it. The weapon of the Comanche was total destruction and ugly death, so they could not complain if it was turned against them. He felt no pity, no sorrow, nothing. He just stood and watched the flames and hoped that Nix would do what he wanted him to do. What happened to the Indians was irrelevant.

Koh-eet-senko and his warriors were the first to see the smoke and recognize its source. Every prairie-savvy rider knows that the only way to fight a running prairie fire is to get the hell away from it, and there are no more prairie-savvy riders than the Comanches. They knew, even if Nix's men did not, that a slight increase in the strength of the wind would send those flames searing across the land at the speed of a galloping horse. They were far too much realists to take the chance of that. Forgetting the promised rewards, forgetting the fugitive whose tracks they had found, forgetting everything except the need to get their families and their possessions out of the path of the fire, the Comanche warriors racked the heads of their ponies around and streamed away in the direction of the encampment. Behind them, in front of Nix and his deserted riders, the long line of flames marched on.

Nix stilled his frightened, curvetting horse, cursing the fleeing Indians, cursing the advancing flames and his own luck until he ran out of curses and stopped, realizing the folly of cursing what was beyond his or any man's control. This fire was no accident. It was Angel, and that meant Angel had seen them and knew they were coming. It meant other things, too. It meant the man had somehow gained access to the stockade. How he had done so without being killed by Yat Sen, Hercules Nix could not imagine. Yet it looked as if there was no other explanation, which in turn meant that somehow, Angel had killed the Oriental, for Nix knew that Yat Sen would never have let the American live.

'Boss?' Des Elliott said anxiously. 'That fire is gettin' awful damned close.'

Nix looked up, shaking off thoughts of doom. Elliott was right. The flames were noticeably nearer, and the sky was filled with tiny floating bits of burned grass that fell like black snow. The flames were already close to the treeline below the Comanche camp, and Nix thought he could see moving dots amid the billowing smoke as the Indians fled the relentless fire. He mantled himself with determination. If Angel had thought the firing of the land a master-stroke, he might yet find it a two-edged one.

He turned to Dooley Watson.

'You!' he snapped. 'Get over there, to the Comanche camp. Find Koh-eet-senko. Tell him that the man who started the fire is at the stockade. Tell him I said if he wants vengeance, to meet me across the river at the dry ford. Tell him I said if we take the man, he can have him. He can do whatever he likes with him. Tell him that!'

'You think he'll listen?' Watson asked dubiously.

'He'll listen!' Nix shouted, putting on a confident face he didn't truly believe in. 'He'll be as mad as a hornet. His horses will all be stampeded. He's lost his camp, his possessions, all his plunder from the raid. Probably a few of his people as well. He'll want revenge for that, so we'll tell him he can have our Angel!'

'But I thought you–?' Elliott said.

'Of course,' Nix said. 'But we won't tell that black-faced bastard that, will we?'

Elliott grinned and as he did, Nix slapped Watson's horse across the haunch. The animal jumped into a run, and thundered off at a tangent toward the Comanche camp. Nix nodded, as if satisfied.

'All right,' he said. 'We'll pull back across the river. Wait for Koh-eet-senko. Then with him, or without him, we hit the *hacienda*. With everything we've got!'

'You what?' Elliott said, surprised. 'Hit the *hacienda*?'

'Yes!' Nix said, his voice rising to a shout. 'That's where he is, so that's where we'll take him. This time we're not going to mess it up! This time we're going to stop Angel – dead!'

EIGHTEEN

Now it was war.

Before this it had been a jaunt, a manhunt with a known ending of sadistic pleasure, but now it was more than that. Koh-eet-senko wanted vengeance, just as Nix had predicted he would, and he had brought thirty warriors with him, painted for war. Their lances caught fire from the bright sun as they streamed behind their leaders down the western side of the valley. Their warrior brothers were busy shepherding the rest of the Timber People out of their encampment, away from the leaping fire. Although they knew it would eventually burn itself out at the rim of the desert, they also knew there would be no life-support left in its wake. The animals had already fled, fleetly outstripping the humans. Behind the still raging flames lay only scorched earth, stunted roots, shriveled trees. The forest was destroyed, and a dozen Comanches had died fighting to save their homes and their horses. A number of warriors had died when they had dashed into the lake for water with which to fight the flames. Their comrades had watched in superstitious, uncomprehending terror as the men thrashed and screamed and bled and died in the water. Some ran to their rescue, only to fall prey to the razor fangs of the piranha themselves. Others had died beneath blazing, falling trees, and the panicked hoofs of terrified ponies. There would be much grief in the night camp of the *Hoh'ees*. The women would slash their arms and their breasts in ritual tribute to the dead, the men would cut short their hair to mourn their brothers. To avenge them Koh-eet-senko had called his best warriors to his side, and they streamed like cavalry in formation behind the knot of Nix's men, faces painted in broad black stripes of war, outpacing the white men as they forged down the valley.

They bore their best lances, their shining repeating rifles. They all wanted to count *coup* on the body of the man who had brought destruction upon them.

Nix, by subtle signals to his men, let the Indians draw ahead. He had bitter experience of Angel's survival techniques, and anticipated that the man from the Justice Department might have some savage tricks waiting for them. Let Koh-eet-senko and his warriors trigger them. Then Nix would strike his own blow.

Angel watched them coming down the valley. He was on the lookout tower at the northwest corner of the stockade. Below him, inside it, Victoria stood near the window of the machinery room, between wall and stockade, two pieces of wire in her hand, bared of insulation. She stood in shadow, her face a pale blur, dressed in riding breeches and neat English-style jacket, looking for all the world as though she was awaiting the arrival of a groom with her horse, ready for the hunt. Angel grinned at the vanity: Victoria might be going hunting, but it was a larger fox than usual that she would pursue. No one would be happier than she to see the man who had built this valley of death destroyed.

He had pieced together the whole story now.

Nix had given him some clues, and she filled in the gaps. She told him of finding the almost-dead Ernie Hecatt on the trail, of riding for help and seeing that he was nursed back to health. When he recovered, Hecatt – who had told them his name was Nix – insisted on working at the ranch to pay off some of his indebtedness to them. He had gradually won the confidence of old Tom Stacey, Victoria's father, and before long, was helping the old man at the bank in Waco. Gradually – he did everything carefully, without haste – Nix made himself indispensable to the old man. He was always on hand to pour the old man a stiff drink, followed by a stiffer one. Within a year, Tom Stacey couldn't get through the day without at least a quart of whiskey, and his mind was so fuddled that he signed anything Nix put in front of him, did anything Nix wanted him to do. There was one thing Nix wanted more than anything else: and that was Victoria Stacey. When he was ready, he took her, too.

'Then we came here,' Victoria had told him while they worked. 'He brought a builder in, hundreds of Mexicans. He worked them like a madman, like Pharaoh building a tomb. When it was finished, he had them all taken away. Then he brought in the others, Elliott and his men. I was as much a prisoner as if I were in jail. He told me if I ever tried to leave the valley he would come after me, and when he caught me he would give me to the Comanches.'

'It was probably just a threat,' Angel said, more to fill in the silence than anything else. 'No white man would give a white woman to an Indian.'

'It was no threat, Frank,' she said, without emphasis. 'He would have done it. He has the soul of Satan himself: there is no foul thing he would not do.'

The Comanches were moving in battle formation as they came whooping down the valley, their line a long broken V with its point to the rear. In the narrowest arm of the V Angel saw a knot of riders and grinned mirthlessly: Nix might have the soul of Satan, but he also had his cunning. He was letting the Indians take the sting out of any surprises that his foe might have prepared. Well, it make no damned difference to Angel. He gave the signal to Victoria and she touched together the ends of the two wires.

It had been hardly any trouble to work out

the way that the crude switches were linked to pump and filter and battery. There were diagrams on the walls to show the locations of the mines, and Angel had been surprised to discover that there was an inner ring of explosives within the stockade, a last-ditch defense of which Nix had said nothing. He had disconnected all the contacts, and then he and Victoria had gone outside and started digging. The buried bombs were simple, and probably brutally effective. Cast-iron canisters, about the size of a cowpat, maybe four inches deep and packed with explosive. A detonator linked to the battery circuit was made live when the switch was thrown. Above it was a springy steel plate which set off the detonator when it was depressed. Man or horse, whatever triggered the device would be blown to smithereens, and the shrapnel of the case would cut through anything nearby as it whickered into a killing spray. There was one of these devices every yard or so, harmless when disconnected, lethal otherwise. They dug all the ones on the northeastern and southern sides of the stockade and lugged them, sweating and dirty, across to the other side. There Angel buried them, making no real effort to conceal them properly. He didn't have the time for finesse. He ran the wires back to the batteries and connected them up, bypassing the switches. All that was needed to set off the mines was a spark, and Victoria supplied that when she touched together the two bared copper wires.

The Indians were thundering toward the stockade, their ornaments and weapons flashing in the brilliant sun, an awesome line of primitive force. Magnificent, ugly, their bodies painted with ochre and vermilion, decorated with amulets and medicine signs, screaming their ululating attack cry, they were about twenty yards from the stockade when the world blew up in their faces.

There was unimaginable panic.

Horses were blown apart, their riders with them. Others were cut down by the terrible slicing force of fragmented metal, still others smashed to the ground by the sheer power of the blast. Horses stopped dead in their tracks, pitching their riders ten and fifteen feet ahead of them in tumbling, broken bundles. In the pattering descent of metal and stone and swirling dust were softer, wetter, warmer things, all that remained of the comrades of those who crawled on the broken ground life shattered insects, blood streaking the bright paint on their bodies. And now from the lookout tower, Angel poured a random hail of lead into the routed Comanche band, emptying the three pre-loaded Winchesters in a staccato roll of shots. The seeking rain of driving lead hard on the heels of the awful explosion was beyond resistance, and Koh-eet-senko gathered together what was left of his men, shouting at them to pull back to where Nix and his men had pulled their mounts to a safe stop, appalled by the slaughter before them. A couple of Elliott's men yanked out their Winchesters and threw shots at the small figure in the look-out tower, but none of them came near Angel. There wasn't a man in a thousand that could hit a mark at half a mile from the back of a horse, much less an animal made jumpy by the proximity of a huge explosion. He watched now through the same telescope that Hercules Nix had used to observe Angel's entry into the valley. He could see Nix gesticulating furiously at the Indian leader, and the Comanche making angry, chopping movements with his hands. It wasn't difficult to guess what they were arguing about, and Angel watched with grim satisfaction. He had won the first skirmish. The tattered things that lay bloodily broken on the smoking ground below were part of the price the Indians had to pay for their allegiance to Nix. But they were casualties only of the battle. The war was not yet over.

The war party had gathered itself again, and now the white men took the lead. Once again Angel grinned: Koh-eet-senko wasn't buying the same trouble twice, and had insisted that Nix and his men took the van. That was what they'd been arguing about: and it suited Angel's purposes admirably. He hoped he'd estimated Nix's reaction correctly. As the riders regrouped and moved out of range, he saw that they were heading south again, and would come around the southern side of the stockade, between it and the mountains. Nix would know the area on the eastern side of the stockade was mined, including the ground in front of the main gates. He would therefore send his men at the walls on either side of the gates, where they could jump the line of mines, or take one of the corners. He had made his own bet. There were no longer any mines before the main gates. He and Victoria had dug them up and redistributed them among the walls, about four feet from the palisade itself.

'Here we go again,' he muttered, as the swiftly moving line of horsemen rounded the southwestern perimeter of the stockade, about half a mile away from it. He counted them: six white men and twenty-two Indians. It was clear that they had discussed and agreed upon some plan of attack. They wheeled to face the stockade in line abreast, each rider about six yards or so from the one next to him. A second line formed behind the first, slightly more men in it. Eighteen, Angel counted, understanding the ploy. The front line of ten was the fire-drawing line. In the days before repeating rifles, the Indians had always fought like this. They knew that even the best men with guns took almost half a minute to reload: pour in the powder, ram home; ball, ram it home; wadding, ram it; up and ready to fire. So they used to send in a screaming squad of a dozen trick riders to draw the fire of their victims. As these riders came within range of the rifles, they dropped to the defensive side of their thundering ponies avoiding, as often as not, the volley of shots aimed at them. Then, as the defenders fired their rifles, the main force of attacking Indians rolled down upon the target, smashing through its defenses before the men inside could reload.

Nix was trying a variation on the same tactic.

The front line would come in, daring Angel to set off his defensive ring, his counterattack, whatever he had. If he didn't, they would keep on coming, take the wall and prepare the way for the second wave. If he did, the second line would come in like a wave over a safe beach, unscathed. The first line was a suicide squad, and Angel could hear snatches of Comanche death songs across the scorched and empty plain.

Only the earth lasts forever
It is a good day for dying
Only the sun lasts forever
It's a good day to die, brother.

Don't worry, brother, he thought, I'll do my best to oblige, and watched as they kicked their horses into movement. He had reloaded the three Winchesters now, and changed his vantage point to the tower overlooking the main gate. It was a well-built hut of logs, with notches for rifles. He laid the three guns out, ready, holding his fire as they came forward steadily, the horses picking up their feet from a walk into a trot, bright flashes of light glancing from the bits of glass and metal tied to their bits. Five hundred yards. Four. Three, and still Angel held his fire. The Winchester '73 was a good weapon, but anyone expecting accuracy from it at more than two hundred and fifty yards was not only an optimist but a fool due for sad disappointment. Two hundred yards, a hundred and fifty. He checked the lever of the first gun: there was a bullet up the spout. One hundred yards.

The Indians were moving at a canter now, yelling and screaming as they kicked the animals up into a gallop, working the levers of their own rifles. As they came in even closer, as if they had been rehearsing the movement for hours, they veered off, forming a looping, open wheel perhaps sixty or seventy yards in diameter, moving so that at any given moment only one or two of them was within rifle range. As the wheel revolved, it edged constantly closer to the wall of the stockade, a yard or so at a time. The Comanche wheel, they called it. It was one of the most effective tactics ever devised by the horseback Indians, the revolving wheel acting like the blade in a sawmill, edging inexorably closer to its target. At any moment, only a short fast-moving arc went close to the enemy, and as it did, the warriors slid down on the leeward side of their ponies, firing their rifles from beneath the neck of the galloping beasts. Angel dropped one horse, then another. Their riders rolled aside like acrobats, and within the space of moments, ran alongside another warrior, whirled up behind him, and dropped off on the safe far side of the circle. They would come in again on foot when the second wave attacked.

Nearer and nearer they came, until now they were no more than twenty yards from the gate, black charcoaled dust hanging like a gritty curtain above them as they yelled and screamed past. Still Nix held back his reserve, although through the dust Angel could see the Indian leader waving his arms as though to argue for attack.

When the short arc of the wheel was no more than ten yards from the gates, Angel turned loose. He emptied one full magazine and then another and then another as fast as he could pull the trigger, his bullets taking a terrible toll of the game little Comanche ponies. The meaty smacks as his bullets drove into their bodies were sickening, but Angel steeled himself against any semblance of pity. His was a war of total attrition, and he had to use every means at his disposal to reduce the strength of his foe. There were now five dead horses on the scorched ground, and Angel knew that two others had been hit badly enough to render them unserviceable. He also knew that the wheel was making its last few turns. He had seen it before; and he knew what came next.

The line straightened as the thought passed through his mind, and the remaining half-dozen warriors ran their horses straight at the gates, shouting their death songs.

There was no explosion, nothing, and after an infinitesimal faltering, they came on with renewed confidence. They reached the gates and wheeled their ponies around, unhitching saddle ropes and tossing them up to catch the pointed tops of the gateposts. Angel let them do it, holding his fire: he had other plans. The Comanches screeched their triumph and kicked their horses away from the gates. The ropes twanged tight, taut, and the thick gateposts rocked as the ponies threw their weight against the horsehair ropes. Slowly, like some ancient longbow, one of the posts bowed and then, suddenly, with a thunderous crack, it broke off about six feet from the ground. The Comanche ponies lurched away, trailing the broken post behind them, and as they did, the gatepost on the other side came down with a tremendous crash that raised a cloud of the black dust fifteen feet high.

The Comanches cast off the ropes and turned their ponies with savage cries of eagerness as their warrior brothers came up at the gallop, Koh-eet-senko at their head, and the long echoing warcry of the Timber People bouncing off the hills to the south. To their right and left came Hercules Nix's men, reins in their teeth and holding their seat with steely leg thews, cocking the guns held in both ready hands. The dust sifted away from the broken gateway that yawned before them and as it did, the Comanches saw the figure of a man running across the courtyard and gave a screech of delight that was still at its height when Angel touched off the cannon.

Perhaps Koh-eet-senko and his warriors saw the cannon, and perhaps they even had one awful moment to realize what would come next. Even if they did, there was absolutely nothing that they could do. The charging mob of horsemen was forced to come closer together as it came through the broken aperture into the stockade, and even if the Comanche were the finest riders in the world, there were limits to their ability to stop and turn and take avoiding action. Angel had gauged those limits to an inch, making his run like a *banderillero* quartering across the face of the bull. Rammed tight down the throat of the old cannon were as many bits of old metal, nails, screws, bolts, washers, nuts, screws, musket balls, and other hardware as Angel had been able to find. As he thrust the burning taper down its newly cleaned touchhole, the old cannon exploded with a stuttering boom and jumped backward on its carriage, collapsing on one wheel. The rushing mob of Comanches was obscured in a huge billowing cloud of powdersmoke through which whistled the cutting, whispering, deadly load. The flying metal made a roaring *WHoooooooommmmmmmmm!* as it smashed into the packed bodies of the men in the gateway. Angel saw the war party torn apart as if it had been struck by some gigantic, invisible weapon wielded by God's own hand. Horses and men were blown apart, cut down by the terrifying force of the close-range blast, torn to shreds without a moment to comprehend the manner of their awful death. The air was alive with the honey-on-herring stink of blood, and broken things that might have been part of men or animals twitched in the trammeled dirt.

Frank Angel had four shotguns ready.

He walked into the screaming, twisted vision of hell before the muzzle of the smoking cannon and emptied them into anything he saw that moved amid the smoking pall of death. As he emptied the guns he tossed them aside, his face as cold as that of the avenging messenger of Satan. He saw men go down beneath the irresistible smash of the buckshot, once heard the soft buzz of a slug going past his own head as someone tried to fight back. He fired the last barrel of the last gun and threw it down, then turned and ran, calling Victoria's name.

The tattered survivors of the war party had fallen back in total disarray, broken by the jaws of hell into which they had ridden. Of the twenty-eight men who had advanced in the bright sunlight upon the stockade, only seven remained, four of them Comanches. They instinctively ran for the solid shelter of the stockade walls, flattening themselves on the outside of the perimeter. They were still moving away from the awesome shambles of the main gates when Angel's shout to Victoria Nix signaled her to once more touch together two bared wires.

The explosives went off with a stuttering series of bangs, like some enormous hammer striking an equally huge anvil. Angel had wired the mines along the walls in series, so that they went off perhaps half-a-second after each other. Once more the air was filled with the awful whistling hail of deadly metal, once more men fell screaming in gutted agony amid smoke and flame. One of them was the Comanche, Koh-eet-senko. A shard of metal about the size of a banana sliced through his neck at a speed of about seven hundred miles an hour. He never even knew he had been killed. The soft sibilant sound of dirt sifting back to earth was followed by a silence that was like the end of all life. Nothing moved. The surviving men stood mute, paralyzed with fear and horror. Smoke eddied on the vagrant breeze.

'Enough, for Christ's sake!' Des Elliott whispered. His face was blackened by smoke, and one of his arms was gashed where the fragment of metal which had decapitated Koh-eet-senko had touched him in passing. He looked at Hercules Nix with naked fear in his eyes. Nix's clothing hung on him in filthy tatters, blood smeared on his face like Comanche war paint. His eyes were empty, insane. Saliva dribbled from slack lips.

Elliott looked around him. There were grisly dead everywhere the eye moved. The skull-faced Hisco, one side of his face a raw pulp of broken flesh, touched his arm and pointed with his chin at the only two Comanches left alive. Their eyes were wide with terror, and they were already inching away from the stinking pile of broken flesh that was all remaining in this world of their warrior brothers. Elliott nodded: let them go. There was nothing they could do, he could do, anyone could do. Turning to the Indians, he held up his right hand, palm vertical, bending all his fingers slightly forward. He pushed his hand out and brought it back, the sign for 'go.' The Comanches needed no second bidding. They nodded dumbly and ran to where some of the ponies had stopped in a milling cluster. They caught up two and swung on to their bare backs, moving away from the carnage without a backward glance. They would keep going until they caught up with what was left of the Timber People.

'Des,' Hisco said.

Elliott turned and saw that Hercules Nix was stumbling through the pile of corpses and dead animals toward the *hacienda*. Elliott watched him narrowly. Had Nix gone mad? Nix was standing in the center of the courtyard, his head to one side in a listening position. Then it came up, and Nix thrust out an arm, pointing to the north.

'There!' he screeched. 'There!'

Now Elliott heard it too, the muted thunder of hoofs. He ran quickly up the wooden ladder to the lookout post on the wall. Two figures on horseback were moving fast up the far side of the river.

'Angel!' Elliott said. 'Angel – and–'

'Victoria!' Nix shouted, and his voice was like a ghost in a deep well. 'Vic-to-ri-aaaaaaaaaaa!'

Elliott and Hisco ran back to where they had left Nix, and as they came near they heard a strange, broken, keening sound. They saw Hercules Nix walking around and around in a tight circle on the patio, stamping his feet like a spiteful child, spittle at the corners of his mouth. Each time he passed the wall of the house he smashed his fist against it. The metal claw was torn, the masking glove stripped off it. It looked obscene.

'Nix!' Elliott said, sharply, but Nix took no notice of him at all. Around and around he went and as he went, he smashed the broken steel hand on the wall, and mouthed something almost unintelligible.

'Horrrrr!' he growled, looking at the sky, the ground, the man in front of him. He got hold of Hisco, who pulled free. 'Errrr I oh. Horrrrrrr!'

'He wants a horse,' Elliott said, suddenly understanding. 'Everything I own for a horse!'

He looked at Hercules Nix, and then at the *hacienda.* He had been inside it a great many times, awed by its casual riches. Gold, silverware, valuable things. Plenty of money, too, no doubt, as well as Nix's collection of fine guns and pistols. A man could make a killing from what was inside. Greed lit his eyes like candlelight and he smiled his twisted smile.

'You heard what the boss said,' he snapped at Hisco. 'Catch him up a horse!'

'Uh?' Hisco said. 'A horse. For him?' Nix looked as if he might have trouble walking.

'Horrrrr!' Nix roared, smashing aside a table with his broken steel claw. 'Horrr!' Then Hisco read the signals in Elliott's face and he nodded.

'Oh, sure,' he said. 'A horse!'

He ran out to where the horses were

standing ground hitched, their eyes rolling at the pervading stink of death. He had trouble getting the animal past the piled corpses in the gateway, but he managed it, and brought it to where Nix still made his mad circles. Nix looked up and his wild eyes focused. He snatched the reins out of Hisco's hand, knocking the skull-faced man asprawl.

'Horrrr!' Nix said, clawing clumsily at the horn of the saddle with his useless artificial hand. Elliott stepped forward and gave him a boost, and without a look, Nix snatched the animal's head around and jammed his spurs into its side. The two men watching saw that there was a wide gap in the northern side of the stockade – obviously the one through which Angel and Victoria Nix had ridden. Nix rocketed through it now, hitting a gallop by the time he had gone fifty yards. Des Elliott flicked a gob of Nix's spittle off his grimy sleeve and looked at Hisco with a grinning leer.

'Well,' he said. 'He offered everything he owned, didn't he?'

Hisco grinned back without need to answer, and the two of them went into the house. They stood in the ornate living room, putting a mental price on everything they could see: the fine collection of rare guns, the antique silver in its oak cabinet, the rich carpets and valuable furniture. They were still licking their lips over their booty when the long fuse that Frank Angel had lit as he and Victoria made their escape reached the explosives, and blew Hercules Nix's *hacienda* to bits.

NINETEEN

'Not far now,' Angel said, trying for a grin.

But it didn't fit: he didn't feel much like smiling as he pulled the horse to a stop at the crest of a long low hill. What he felt like was rolling into his blankets and sleeping around the clock, a bone-deep tiredness that made his long muscles ache, his eyes gritty, his mouth taste sour. He scanned the land to the south behind them. A fat black pillar of smoke climbed from the ruins of Hercules Nix's stronghold. The *hacienda*, pivot of Nix's kingdom, was destroyed, and with its destruction the whole valley would die. The river would cease to flow, the lake beside what had been the Comanche camp dry up, the swamp disappear. The wildlife and the vegetation would depart or perish. Perhaps one day, a thousand years from now, some roaming archaeologist would find the fossil of one of the ugly piranha, and rush back to whatever civilization existed then, proclaiming a new theory of evolution based on finding fish in the high plateaus of Texas. It wasn't much to hang a grin on, but it would have to do.

What of Nix – was he dead? There was no sign of the dust of pursuit. After the merciless destruction in the stockade, was there anyone left to pursue them? There was irony in the way that Nix's stronghold had in the end been the instrument of his destruction. He had built it to be impregnable to every kind of attack except the one that had finally come about, his premise of inviolability removed by the simple reversal of position, the unexpected result of a hunted animal becoming the hunter.

Bullfighters will tell you that apart from the normal dangers of their profession, the one they fear most is one little known to most spectators. No matter how long, how successful, how unbroken their string of killings, matadors share the nightmare that one day a bull will erupt from the *toril* who has been 'educated.' Matadors work on the premise that, all things being equal, the *lidia* will end with the predestined death of the bull, just as Nix had begun his hunt certain of how it would end, improvising only the means. Matadors fear that bull which has, without their knowledge, fought a man before. No matter how stringent the precautions of the breeders, no matter how careful the selection of his *cuadrilla*, sooner or later the matador is going to get a bull who's been run by some kid swinging a coat in a moonlit field. Lots of the kids get hurt, many more don't. They have their fun and then hop back over the fence, head for the *cantina* to boast of their prowess. In a week they have forgotten the bull, but the bull has forgotten nothing. He learns very fast, and what he learns he remembers when he faces the matador. Which is why such an animal is feared. He does not fight by the rules. He ignores the cape. He goes without warning or mercy for the man.

Hercules Nix had met such an animal. Instead of fighting by the rules, it had ignored them, and destroyed him as mercilessly as the rogue bull guts the *torero*.

Masking his exhaustion, Angel glanced at Victoria Nix. Her face and clothes were as sweat-stained and dusty as his own, and deep in her eyes he could see the controlled fear still lingering. Until she knew for sure that Nix was dead it would remain there, and there was nothing Angel could do about it. After the carnage in the stockade, Nix ought to be dead: but that didn't offer a guarantee that he was. Again, Angel scanned the land behind them. He had no way of knowing the full extent of the destruction he had effected. He only knew what he had done to bring it about.

He had piled together the mines dug up from the inside defense perimeter, laying them at strategic points throughout the *hacienda*. He placed them for maximum compressive effect: between the stinking acid-filled batteries, inside the casing of the silent pump, on the shelved walls of the deep well. He found a big crate of dynamite in the machine room and linked these bundles to the circuit, placing them beneath the joints of supporting buttress of floor or ceiling, and at the corners of the walls where they would do the most damage. From all these he ran a long fuse to the gap which he had opened in the stockade beside the river. Two horses, ready-saddled, stood waiting, and as Angel ran across the stockade that one last time, he shouted Victoria's name and she lit the slow-burning fuse. Angel had gauged it for about ten minutes but it took only eight for the fizzing knot of fire to reach the detonator and blow the *hacienda* and the men in it to Kingdom Come. Now Angel's gaze traversed the blackened, scorched land he had fired earlier. It was empty, useless now: with the water system destroyed, it would remain barren. No Comanche tribe would ever use it for a camp again, no unarmed, naked men run through it seeking sanctuary that did not exist. Death itself was a just visitation upon what had been the kingdom of a madman.

'Frank!' Victoria said, all at once, her voice tight with fear. She was pointing at the land below and behind them and when he saw what she was pointing at, a long, soft sigh seeped from his lips. Dust rose in a thin spiral, a long way behind them. The pursuit had begun again, and if there was pursuit it meant that Nix was not dead. If he were dead, his bandits would not bother to carry out his revenge. They would care only for their own survival. Angel cursed himself for having abandoned Nix's telescope in the stockade. It would have been useful to know the strength of the pursuit, but he had no intention of waiting until it was close enough for him to count them.

'All right,' he said. 'Let's get going.'

She needed reassurance, but he wasn't going to lie to her. The fawn-frightened look was back in her eyes for real now, and he reached over and touched her hand, gently. Her hair was all blown loose and hung down her back in auburn waves. Even grimy and a long way from home, she was a beautiful woman. She smiled, but her heart wasn't in it.

'Good girl,' he told her. 'You'll be fine.'

Then they headed down the long slope toward the north, toward the now-visible barrier of the thornbreaks ahead. In them lay the last remnant of Nix's power, the guards at the Portal. They would not know what had happened at the other end of the valley, nor would they believe it unless they saw it. So there was no margin for error at all.

The pursuer was Nix, and Nix alone.

He thundered in pursuit of the fugitives without true consciousness of his own motivation, identity, or destination. The delicate links between his reason and his action centers were destroyed, the brain functioning like a misfiring engine, synapses gaping. The man pursuing Angel and Victoria Nix was insane.

Die, die, they'll all die, I'll kill them, all of them, both? Slowly without mercy, they must die and they will die. They will die and I will laugh and they will see me laughing as they die. They? Two of them. Her. Especially her. The other one. Him, is it him? He's the one. They have to die. It must be. They'll die, all of them, they'll all die, I'll kill them, all of them.

The thoughts ran through Nix's broken mind like water, unconsciously impelled, without volition. He spurred his flagging horse unmercifully, not even aware that he had raked the animal's body to bloody tatters with the wicked rowels of his silver spurs. It would not have made any difference had he known: the only thing that mattered to the man was pursuit, movement, revenge. Who, where, why, there were unimportant. They had destroyed everything. It was finished, all gone. There was nothing left except vengeance, and the fearful red thing in his brain goaded him on in quest of it. He thundered up the western side of the valley, the wind whipping away the spittle from his drooling lips. Tortured visions of what he would do when he caught his quarry danced like dervishes behind his eyes. Mad beyond redemption, Hercules Nix careered northward.

TWENTY

The entrance to the Portal was a killing ground.

The cabin stood back at the edge of the thornbreaks, and the area in front of it lay like a table, empty, denuded of every vestige of shrubbery. Nothing, not even a gopher, could have moved over it without being seen, and now Angel was grateful for the time he had spent surveying it earlier. He told Victoria he wanted to try to take the men in the barrack alive: he did not know what infernal devices Nix might have planted along the narrow trail to freedom. Now Victoria Nix rode out of the trees on his signal and moved up toward the hut. As she came into sight, a man came out, walking in a slouch toward her horse, his right hand trailing a shotgun. A cigarette drooped from his lips, and he looked at Victoria with a puzzled frown.

'Miz Nix,' he saluted. 'What you doin' up here on your ownsome?'

'What is your name?' Victoria said frostily, ignoring his question and regarding the man as if he were some loathsome new species of bug she'd found in her linen closet. He was no oil painting: his stubble was at least a week old, and his clothes looked as if he'd never changed them since the day he put them on.

'Sweddlin, ma'am,' he muttered, scuffing shabby boots. 'Lee Sweddlin.'

'Are you alone here? Where is everyone?'

'They done took off to help the Ol' – beg your pardon, the boss, ma'am,' Sweddlin said. 'There's just the two of us here, me an' Sanson.'

'Tell him to come out here.'

'Uh, ma'am, we got orders not to–'

'Do you defy me, sir?' Victoria said frigidly, her eyebrows climbing an astonished inch. 'Do you dare to defy me?'

'Uh, ah, no, ma'am,' Sweddlin said hastily. He raised his voice to a cracked shout. 'Hey, Kit, c'mon out here, will ya?'

The door of the shack opened and another man came out. He was meatily built, the body of an athlete gone to seed. A heavy paunch hung over his belt and like Sweddlin he looked as if he hadn't shaved for a week.

'I can see,' he said, testily. 'I can see.'

'Good,' Angel said behind him. 'Then if you turn around real slow you'll see this gun I'm pointing at you.'

Sweddlin tensed slightly, staring at Victoria as if she had committed an unutterable blasphemy. She saw him think about using the shotgun still held at trail in his right hand.

'No,' she said. 'Don't do that. We don't want to kill you.'

Sweddlin nodded and as if coming to a much-considered decision, let go of the shotgun, and slowly raised his hands. He wasn't the type to buck odds. Not life-or-death odds, anyway. He'd stayed alive this long by knowing when not to fight, and he wasn't about to spoil a perfect track record now. Behind him Sanson nodded and spat into the dirt. But he raised his hands as well, turning slowly to face Angel.

It was the work of only moments to disarm them, and of minutes to tell them what had happened in the valley. Angel used short, explicit words and brief graphic sentences. He told them how many men were dead for certain, and the names of those he knew. He told them how those men had died and why.

He told them about the slaughter in the stockade, and what he had done to destroy it. He told it very convincingly and they believed him. Maybe they weren't convinced by the details of his outline. Maybe what convinced them was that he was here, and that Victoria Nix was with him. Sweddlin and Sanson both knew that Nix never allowed her to leave the *hacienda* alone. Either Nix accompanied her personally, or she was shadowed by the deadly Oriental, Yat Sen. When Angel capped his story by showing them his belt-hidden badge, with its screaming eagle encircled by the legend *Department of Justice*, any fight they might have had in them drained out like bathwater. Sanson was foxier than his partner: he tried for a bargain.

'Lissen, Angel,' he said. 'We go along, tell you how to get out, what's in it for us?'

'I turn you loose when we get clear,' Angel said. 'Forget I ever saw you.'

'And if we don't?'

'I'd say that would be ... inadvisable,' Angel said, almost reflectively. 'Because what I'd do would be to herd you two in front of me all the way through the breaks so that whatever happened, you'd be the first ones it happened to.'

The two of them looked at him for a long, long moment.

'You could be bluffin',' Sanson said.

'That's right.'

'You'd do that, what you said? Go through the breaks with us in front?' Sweddlin asked, his voice tailing away weakly when he saw the look on Angel's face.

'Yes, you would,' he said. 'Listen, Kit, tell him. Or I sure as hell will.'

Sanson nodded, and began to explain the system of switches that primed the mined road that ran through the breaks. It was similar to the one back at the *hacienda*, powered by the same huge, stinking battery.

'Then there's a system of signal flags,' Sanson said. 'Two flags, one red, one black. Red means whoever is coming through is OK. Black–'

'I can guess,' Angel said. 'What happens then?'

'When he sees the flag go up the pole, Chris Holmes – that's the guy at the other end – he hoists a red flag, too. That means he's switched off at his end. Otherwise, wouldn't make no difference if we was switched off or not, the mines would still be primed.'

'He's got a lookout platform up there,' Sweddlin added. 'He can check on who's comin' through. He doesn't like the look of 'em, he can get back inside and throw the switch anyway, blow the road up in your face.'

'It's damn near foolproof,' Sanson said, and Angel nodded, moved in spite of himself to admire the dark brain that had planned all this. He listened as Sweddlin described the steel plate set beneath the dirt of the road that depressed a bell, which told the man at the far side to check on who was coming through. If he did not know them, he challenged them, and if they gave the wrong reply, he simply threw his switch. There was no way they could get to him before he did so. As Sanson had said, it was almost foolproof, and he thanked the instinct which had told him to take these guards alive.

'All right,' he told Sweddlin. 'Get the red flag hoisted. And make sure you do it exactly right.'

'I'll do it right,' Sweddlin said anxiously. 'Don't you worry.'

'Don't you worry about me worrying,' Angel said. 'Get at it.'

Sweddlin clambered up a ladder into a sort of loft, and after a moment Angel heard the squeak of rope pulleys. After a moment,

Sweddlin appeared in the aperture and beckoned him up. Angel handed a sixgun to Victoria, and picked up Sweddlin's shotgun.

'Keep an eye on him,' he said, gesturing at Sanson. 'If he blinks, shoot his face off.'

Victoria nodded, trying for a smile that slid off her face before it got a proper grip, but she took the heavy weapon and cocked it. Sanson flinched visibly at the sound.

In the loft Sweddlin handed a spyglass to Angel and pointed off to the north. Through the glass, Angel could see the flutter of a bright square of scarlet from a pole that thrust up above the ragged top of the thornbreaks.

'All right,' he said. 'Let's go. And you boys listen to me – don't do anything that might prove fatal.'

'Don't worry, mister,' Sweddlin said anxiously. 'We don't aim to doublecross you.'

'I plan to be sure of it,' Angel said coldly as they climbed onto their horses and moved into the shadowed breaks. The trail curved right and then left, leading between the high stands of faceless chokethorn and briar, eerily cool and dark and silent. Glancing at the narrow strip of sky above his head, Angel estimated it would be dark in maybe two hours. A quick scan of the horizon with

Sweddlin's spyglass had revealed no sign of the pursuers, but he knew they were coming and he knew that if the two mercenaries got as much as an inkling that help was on the way they would turn to treachery as naturally as they opened their eyes in the morning.

They moved at a steady trot through the shadowed trees. Once in a while, they startled some creature in the dark depths of the breaks, and heard it crashing through the tangle in panicked flight. Victoria Nix rode in back, close to Angel, her shoulders hunched as though against a chill, her face set and pale.

It took them fifteen minutes to get to the place where a huge white blaze scarred a fallen log beside the trail. Sweddlin reined in as he got level with it. The trail stretched straight as an arrow ahead of them, and disappeared up ahead around a bend. It was quite wide here, and Angel could see the spidery outlines of a look-out platform in the far high distance. Sweddlin stood up in the stirrups and waved his Stetson around his head three times to the right, and three times to the left.

'OK,' he said, and gigged his horse into motion. Ten minutes later, they saw the trail widen and as suddenly as the breaks had closed in on them at the start, they ended. There was a clearing lit by the long rays of the afternoon sun, and in it a barrack hut identical with the one they had just left. As the quartet rode into the open space, a man eased out of the doorway of the hut, a shotgun across his arm. He looked edgy, a little tense, and Angel felt a cold moment of unease.

'Lee, Sanson,' the man nodded, not coming nearer to them. 'What brings you over here? Howdy, Miz Nix, I didn't see–'

'It's all right,' Victoria said, but her voice cracked, and the man sensed the tension in it. His eyes swung immediately to the only stranger in the setup, and the shotgun followed the movement, twin barrels coming up trained unwaveringly on Angel's belly.

'Somebody better tell me what the hell is goin' on here,' he growled, 'or somebody is goin' to get his brains blowed out.'

The air was still, electric with held violence. It was Victoria Nix who dispersed with a casual sound of irritated impatience. She hitched the head of her horse around so that it was between Holmes and Angel and looked down imperiously at Holmes.

'Holmes,' she said, and there was a whip in

her voice that brooked no refusal. 'Help me down.'

Holmes moved automatically to obey. He was a paid gun and there were few things he would balk at doing without so much as batting an eyelid, but he knew a damned sight better than to disobey Hercules Nix's wife. She might be a hoity-toity bitch who treated everyone like so much dirt, but an insult to her was an insult to Nix and an insult to Nix meant death. He extended his hand, and helped her down from the saddle and he was turning around when Angel stuck the long barrel of his Peacemaker into Holmes's ear.

'Don't even sweat,' Angel said softly.

'Aaaah, shit!' Holmes said, looking at Sweddlin and Sanson as though they had just admitted to assassinating Lincoln. Angel grinned. It was funny the way these empty-minded killers used betrayal and treachery as their everyday coin, yet somehow felt tricked when paid in their own money.

'Drop the shotgun,' Angel said. 'Relax.'

'Relax, he says,' Holmes sneered, letting the weapon fall with a soft thud to the ground. 'What the hell is all this, anyway?'

'Tell him,' Angel said to the two Nix riders.

Sweddlin and Sanson nodded, and told Holmes the same story that Angel had told them. If anything, they made it more convincing and bloody than he had done, and when they were through, Holmes looked at Angel in a new way. He shook his head, as though finding it hard to believe.

'You did all that?' he asked Angel. 'Alone?'

'Would I lie to you?' Angel said, with a sardonic grin.

'It's a possibility,' Holmes said, just as derisive. 'Who the hell are you, anyway?'

'He's Federal Law, Chris,' Sweddlin said. 'Department of Justice.'

'Oh, beautiful,' Holmes said, his tone that of a man whose best cards in a high-stakes game are deuces. His face fell further when Angel showed him the badge.

'Department of Justice,' Holmes read, dispiritedly. 'Terrific.'

Angel said nothing, just letting the worry build in Holmes's mind. He was smarter than his two comrades, and knew the consequences of being taken by Federal Law. Holmes had no illusions about what he was: a paid killer, worthless as a citizen, beyond redemption as a human being. He stank of killing for money, but like a buffalo hunter, he had gotten used to the stink.

Angel let the man sweat: the manner of Holmes's eventual death was a predictable as what he would do next. He was expecting Angel to take them in, and he was thinking about years and years in the slammer: ergo, he would try to make some kind of deal.

'Listen,' he said. 'Sanson an' Sweddlin, they played along with you. I'm doin' the same. What's–?'

'Forget it!' Angel said. 'I'm going to turn you loose.'

Holmes's face brightened perceptibly, and he looked at the other two. They nodded. 'That's what he told us, Chris,' Sweddlin said.

'One thing,' Angel said, the coldness of his voice taking the smile of relief off of Holmes's face. 'I want you long gone out of Texas. Keep going until you get someplace where nobody ever heard of the Department of Justice, because if I ever hear you boys are back in circulation, I'm going to come after you and bring you in. And I'll throw away the key, savvy?'

The three men nodded. It was a better deal than they had any right to hope for and they knew it. In their world, losers got a bullet in the gut or the back of the head. There were no nice guys. This cold-eyed bastard had destroyed Hercules Nix single-handed. By definition he was not the kind of man wanted on his back-trail.

'All right,' Holmes said. 'Can we move out now?'

'Now's a good time,' Angel said. 'Get your pony.'

'How about our guns?'

Angel just looked at him, and Holmes got a stubborn look on his face.

'Lissen, mister, you can't send us out alone on these plains without a gun of some kind!' Holmes said. 'There's Comanch' out there. An' Kiowa! They'd slit our throats soon as look if they saw we didn't have guns.'

'No guns,' Angel said.

'Well, hell, then shoot us here and be done with it!' Holmes spat defiantly. 'You're killing us sure the other way, and me, I'd as soon die right here on ground I know.'

'Frank...?' Victoria Nix said hesitantly.

'All right,' Angel said. 'A carbine each. No hand guns.'

'Deal,' Holmes said. 'I'll get mounted.'

He slouched over to the corral. Sweddlin and Sanson walked their horses toward him as he swung up. And Angel watched all three of them for the slightest hint of treachery.

It was a damned good job he did.

As Holmes swung into the saddle, a sudden sound shattered the soft silence of the approaching dusk. There was no mistaking what it was – the insistent clamor of an alarm bell. Simultaneously, the drum of approaching hoofs became audible. Someone was coming along the trail through the breaks. Holmes heard the sound and overreacted, and his action triggered the other two into treacherous reflex violence.

'Bastard!' Holmes yelled at Angel. 'You tricked us!'

He pulled his horse around in a rearing turn, yanked the carbine in the saddle scabbard out and levering it onehanded. Sweddlin and Sanson split, Sweddlin diving out of the saddle with his own carbine, rolling as he thumbed shells into the magazine, while Sanson swung down and dived in a desperate attempt to reach the shotgun that Chris Holmes had dropped in the dust. Angel ignored them, keeping every atom of his concentration on Holmes. Any man who used his horse as a shield that way, and that fast, also knew enough to shoot damned well. It was a smart, killer's move – perhaps one man in ten thousand could hit the few exposed parts of a rider's body if he reared his horse like that, under pressure and fast – and Holmes grinned in confident glee as he pulled his trigger. His last thought was that he'd killed Angel and then Angel's unerring sixgun bullet smashed through his mouth and blew his skull apart in a spraying pink mist of bone and brain. Holmes's bullet chunked a spout of earth a foot high out of the ground near Angel's foot, but the Justice Department man was already moving in a crouched right turn, laying the sixgun across his forearm and putting three bullets in a close cluster below Kit Sanson's right armpit as the man closed his hand on the shotgun. The heavy bullets rolled Sanson over as dead as a brained mackerel, and Lee Sweddlin, who was just bringing the carbine up to use it, found himself gaping into the yawning muzzle of Angel's weapon. He screamed like a gutted wolf, pants staining with his own terror, and dropped the carbine, throwing it away from him as he turned and ran. He was a dead easy target, but Angel did not fire, couldn't do it. Sweddlin careered across the face of the breaks, and turned sharp left into the gap leading to the trail back.

Angel was already running, but not in pursuit of Sweddlin. He ran up the ladder to the lookout platform like a squirrel, snatching up the spyglass that lay on the bench and focussing on the long, straight, narrow cut between the close-growing trees. For a moment he could see nothing, and then all at once his sight was filled with the insane, contorted face of Hercules Nix. He was quite alone, his arm rising and falling like an automaton as he relentlessly thrashed the dying horse with his whip. The animal was covered in blood from withers to chest, hide stripped by the terrible spurs. Its eyes wept blood and it was all but dead on its feet.

Angel threw down the spyglass and ran to the edge of the platform. Victoria was at the foot of the ladder staring up at him.

'Frank?' she called. 'Frank, how many of them are there?'

'It's Nix!' he shouted. 'It's Nix, and he's by himself!'

'Alone?' she shouted.

He didn't answer her. His mind was already emptied of everything except what he had to do next. He had to get down to the ground, snatch up the shotgun lying alongside Kit Sanson's crumpled corpse, and run to where Nix would come out of the gap between the breaks. He wanted to be there, shotgun ready, for Jaime Lorenz, for Tyrrell, for all the men the oncoming madman had cut down.

He came down the ladder face forward, like a sailor, and whirled around toward the hut, intent on the gun. There was no sign of Victoria and he wondered where she had gone. As he snatched up the shotgun he saw a movement inside the hut, and for a moment he could not believe what he had seen. He ran to the doorway of the hut and barged in. She was standing by the huge black lead-acid batteries and her hand was on the H-shaped switch that would make the mines beneath the trail live.

'No!' he shouted. 'Victoria, no!'

'Oh, yes,' she whispered. Her face was like a death-mask. 'Yes, oh, yes!'

And she threw the switch.

TWENTY-ONE

Angel lay on the bed in his apartment.

Downstairs, he could hear Mrs Rissick bustling about in her kitchen, and the faint sound of traffic drifted up from F Street. It was already winter in Washington, cold and damp in the night, dark before six. Right now there was a weak, watery sun up in an uncertain sky and it cast long stripes of light across the carpet of the room. A million dust motes danced in the beams and Angel let his lassitude drift over him, like warm waves on a tropic shore. It was an old and familiar feeling, not unwelcome: the fatigue that always followed the deep physical and emotional drainage of engagement. It always came when you knew everything was over, the veins and arteries sutured, the dead buried, and the ties formed in the copper-smelling heat of action finally cut. It was a time when he went over his own actions again and again, reviewing them in his mind, replaying them in slow motion to see if there had been any alternative open. There were men in the department who enjoyed the killing, he knew; but he was not one of them. He never failed to wonder whether it was justified, and even if it was, what it proved. It didn't ever prove a damned thing to kill a man, yet you rarely got any choice. It was acceptable on that basis. Not delightful, not admirable, not a thrill, but acceptable. What was unacceptable was where you made a choice and didn't know if it had been the right one. Those were the ones that tore you apart.

'Victoria,' he said aloud, thinking of her.

They had ridden away from the valley in silence, burying no dead and not looking back. In time they had come to Madura. It was black dark by the time they reached the town's only hotel. Angel asked for and got the two largest rooms in the place. He left Victoria in one of them while he went to the sheriff's office. She was calm, compliant, and utterly without expression. When he told her to, she stood or walked or ate or drank, acting – to any casual observer – almost completely normal. Certainly no more abnormal than a lot of folks who were what they called slow on the uptake. Only someone who had seen her before, someone who knew her – like Angel – saw the empty deadness behind the eyes. He knew that whatever dam was holding back the reaction, it had to burst soon. It had held precariously ever since she had thrown the switch at the hut outside the entrance to Nix's valley, but it wouldn't hold a hell of a lot longer, and he didn't want her to be alone when it did. So he hurried through his conversation with the sheriff, leaving that worthy greatly worried, sweatily uneasy, and anything but completely informed about the events that had taken place in Nix's kingdom. Angel's explanations – and his promise to enlarge upon them the next day – were just this side of perfunctory, and the string of instructions he left with the sheriff meant that worthy would have to do without most of his sleep that night. The sheriff banged his fist on the desk with anger – but not until his visitor was gone.

When Angel got back to the hotel, Victoria was still sitting in the same chair, staring with neither expression nor interest at the roses-and-rhubarb wallpaper on the opposite wall. When he told her she must get some sleep, she nodded, and allowed herself to be led into the bedroom like a child. He waited until she was in bed, then crept in to check on her. She was already asleep.

The next day he left the hotel while Victoria was still asleep and spent most of the morning with the sheriff. A sheaf of telegraph messages in the department's simple next-letter code lay on that worthy's desk, and he pushed them across to his visitor with a dyspeptic snort.

'What'n'the hell is all that mumbo-jumbo, anyways?' he asked aggrievedly.

Fine thing when a man couldn't even find out what was going on and tell his cronies over a beer in the saloon later. Angel gave him a couple of halfway decent lies to chew on, and digested the real instructions from the Attorney-General, who had agreed to his proposal that he stay with Victoria Nix until she came out of her withdrawn state. A troop of Texas Rangers was going to check out the valley, and would report back in due course. Meanwhile, Angel could file a full report when he got back to Washington, which should not be later than twenty-one days from today's date. He smiled at the instruction, seeing the old man giving it. Then he went back to the hotel.

Victoria was up and dressed, sitting in the chair, waiting for nothing in particular.

'Victoria,' he said gently. 'It's all over now. I've made arrangements for us to leave tomorrow. Head for San Antonio and take a train from there to New Orleans. You said your father's lawyer was in New Orleans, didn't you?'

'Yes,' she said without interest. 'New Orleans.'

'Do you want something to eat?'

'Yes.'

That evening, the sheriff's wife, an apple-faced woman with the bright blue eyes of a child, brought them a cooked cold chicken and a bottle of dry white California wine she said she'd been saving for a special occasion.

'Poor mite,' she said, looking at Victoria. 'She looks real peakit.'

It was obvious she wanted to stay and ask questions, but after a polite while Angel shooed her off like a chicken, and asked the desk clerk to lay a table for them in the dining room. The wine was sharp-tasting and pleasant, and it brought some of the life back into Victoria's eyes. She hardly touched any of the chicken, but absently sipped the wine as Angel kept topping her glass. When the clerk cleared away the dishes, her eyes were already cloudy with sleep, and by the time they got upstairs, it was all she could do to stay awake.

'Frank,' she said unexpectedly. 'It's so hard to find words–'

He touched her soft lips with a gentle forefinger, and shook his head. 'Then don't try,' he said quietly. He opened the door to her room. 'Just sleep. It will wait until tomorrow.'

'Yes,' she said. Her eyes were as wide as a ten-year-old's on Christmas Eve. 'Tomorrow.' She rose on tip-toe and kissed his cheek, light as the touch of a snowflake. Then she went into the room and closed the door. Angel stood for a moment in the corridor, and then went into his own room. He didn't give a damn for the conventions of Madura, or the clucks of its old ladies. If Victoria's barriers cracked he wanted to be able to get to her quickly, and he had told the room clerk to leave the communicating door between the rooms unlocked.

'You bet, Chief,' the clerk had grinned, and Angel had restrained the urge to slap the leer off his pimply face. Instead he went over to the washstand and when the clerk held out his hand for the expected tip, Angel put the bar of soap in it.

'What's this, Chief?' he asked, puzzled.

'Take it downstairs,' Angel suggested, 'and wash your mind out with it.'

For a moment, the clerk looked as if he might retort, but then he saw the look in Angel's eyes and decided to swallow the unspoken jibe. This stranger might be an ungrateful sonofa, but he also looked like the kind of ungrateful sonofa who'd kick your ass through your earhole if you told him so. He backed out, and Angel smiled as he locked the door behind the narrow leer. He undressed now, grinning again at the recollection, and lay on the bed. His mind kept going back to the last moments in the hut at the mouth of the valley, Victoria with her hand on the lever, eyes like the vengeance of Kali. The black batteries had looked like the tombs of some forgotten civilization, she one of its reincarnated priestesses as she pulled the switch. There was a long, long silence of perhaps three seconds, and then a stuttering roll of sound, an interrupted thunder that flattened the eardrums for a moment and then passed like a soft sighing wind. Angel had stood, poised for an action there was no point now in taking, and watched as, slowly, slowly, seeming to shrink inside herself as she did it, Victoria had released her pent-up breath.

'There,' she had whispered. 'There.'

Angel saw what was happening to her and he moved across the hut, his hand outstretched, some words of reassurance forming in his mind. She whirled around like a cat, her eyes blazing.

'Keep away from me!' she rasped. 'Don't you *touch* me!'

'I wasn't going to–'

'Keep your consolation!' she snapped, her voice as tight as a cello string. 'I wanted to kill him, do you hear me?'

'Yes,' he said. 'I hear you. It's all right.'

'I'm glad,' she shouted. 'Glad, glad! I hope

his black soul rots forever in Hell!'

He said no more then. It was as good an epitaph for Hercules Nix as any, and probably better than the man had deserved. He went out of there and got the horses, and when he came back she was standing staring out the window with the empty look she had had ever since. Fifteen minutes later they rode away without a backward glance. Smoke from the fire he had started belched from the door and windows of the hut. Within an hour it would be a charred ruin. The desert could have all that was left of the mad dream of Ernie Hecatt, alias Hercules Nix.

It was warm and close in the hotel room, but after a while, he slept. Her soft warmth awoke him, and he opened his eyes as she reached for him in the darkness, her face wet with tears, body heaving with sobs that would not break. Almost soundlessly she was saying 'Oh, oh, oh, oh,' over and over, and he knew the dam had finally cracked, knew now that she needed something strong and warm and solid to hang onto. It could be anyone, he told his body; it just happens I'm nearest. So he held her close and he rocked her as he would have rocked a small child afraid of the bogeyman. And as he did the small crack that had brought her seeking comfort widened and finally broke and she sobbed and sobbed as if she had seen the end of the world and had nobody to tell about it.

She cried like that for almost an hour, tears coming from her as if from some bottomless salty source, and then she sniffled, and stopped. She shivered slightly, and her skin turned cold and clammy to the touch. He reached over and drew a blanket up around her naked shoulders, folding her into it, and saying the useless, helpless words a man says to a weeping woman; there, there, never mind, it's all right, there, there now. After a while she seemed to sleep, and he laid her softly on his pillow, easing his own body away from her. As if sensing his intent, she tightened her slender arms around him and muttered a sound that might have been 'no.' He made some more of the gentle shushing sounds, and lay alongside her on the bed, his body aching from the long, rhythmic hours of soothing, rocking. A faint paleness in the sky hinted at the coming dawn, and he felt the coolness of the desert breeze through the open window. He thought that afterward he slept a little, but he was never sure. What he remembered was her awakening slowly, warmth coming from her body, a slow sweet heat like a mist that enveloped him, and her slim bare arms sliding around his body as her soft sweet lips touched his face. There was one long moment of waiting, a moment when he rationalized and told himself that the affirmation of life is a primal force in all of us. There are innumerable stories of survivors of some awful disaster clinging together with a passion that springs from instinct and not affection, from the very depths of the being. It might be some kind of compulsion put in us by a knowing Nature to ensure the survival of the species, or nothing more than a desperate need to feel all the strong and reassuring thunders of life, the sharing of the body's best gifts. It was not love and he knew it, but the moment came and went and with it went the will to draw away. After that there was only the long litheness of her, the sweet, scented depths of her, the quick, half-surprised inhalation of pleasure as they joined and the rising crescendo of their need for each other. Up into some dark night beyond the night, totally present in each other, completely absent from self, lovers and strangers simultaneously, they lived and then died the long, long moment that ended in a soft, slow curve of arriving back, silent and rewarded.

After a while, she started to move as if leaving, and he caught her arm. She turned her body back toward him, soft breasts warm and damp against his own moistened body.

'Would you leave without saying a word?' he said softly. 'I want to talk to you, get to know you now.'

'It's – all right,' she said gently. 'You don't – have to.'

So she stayed and they talked until the dawn painted the window pink and then they slept. That day they smiled a lot as they packed, and rented a buggy to take them to San Antonio. From there they took a train to New Orleans. Each day they were there the sadness left her a little, each day she became stronger, smiled more. There was a bloom on her like a fresh peach, a lightness in her step, a firmness to the touch of her. She drew the glances of men in the street, and laughed when Angel glared at them. They lived in an enclosed spectrum of each other, where clocks had no meaning and days had no name. They walked through the world inside a golden haze that excluded everyone else. They found an old restaurant in the Vieux Carrel with real lace tablecloths, old oil lamps, fine French cooking. They ate like castaways and drank chilled Sancerre that tasted of the stones of France. They walked hand in hand beneath wrought-iron balconies and listened to the sweet sad sound of the Negro music from the cellars. All their days were sunny and all their nights were cool and endless. They swam in the soft warm waters of the Gulf, and joined shameless bodies whenever it pleased them to do so. And then one day Victoria told him she was ready to leave New Orleans.

'Good,' he said, grinning. 'Where are we going?'

'No, Frank,' she said. 'I mean alone.'

'Ah. You mean alone.'

What were you supposed to do, he thought. Kick over the table? Punch one of the attentive waiters? Weep or wail or gnash your teeth? She leaned across the table and touched his hand, her fingers like gossamer. He watched the lips that he remembered in hoyden abandon speak words that seemed unreal.

'Darling,' Victoria said. 'You have to let me go now.'

'Why?' he asked. 'Would you like to try to tell me why?'

She nodded, and he saw tears waiting to

be spilled behind her eyes, too. She looked up at the ceiling and drew in a deep breath. Her breasts lifted beneath the thin cotton blouse. The long line of her sweet throat was golden brown from the sun, and somewhere in an echoing empty room in his mind someone said the words 'never again'.

'I love you, Frank,' she whispered, and before he could reply, she put her fingers softly on his lips. 'Before you make the standard required reply, let me say the rest of it. I love you. I love you very much, my dear, but if I walk away from you now, I think I can get over it. It will hurt for a while, but I could do it, and remember you as someone very special, someone I would think of fondly and who would always be very important to me ... if I go now. But if I stay – and I will stay if you ask me to – then I want all of it, Frank. The gold ring and the white dress, the house and the fat babies, everything. I'm that kind of woman, darling. I want that kind of man and that kind of life and I won't settle for less. Do you understand?'

He nodded.

'Then what is it to be?'

Her gaze was intent and searching, and there was a faint tremor of anticipation, or perhaps fear, around the corners of her mouth. He looked at her and she saw the answer and she smiled.

'You are a goddamned fool, Frank Angel,' she said softly.

Now in the shaded quiet of his apartment in the capital city, he heard her voice in the echoing empty room in his mind. She had left New Orleans the next day, and refused to allow him to see her off at the railroad depot. He didn't know where she had gone, or what had happened to her, and he knew he was going to spend the rest of his life wondering whether he'd somehow let the right one, the one it was meant to be, get away. Never again, the voice said.

'Shut up,' he told it, and went into the other room. He poured himself a stiff drink from the bottle on the table. The whiskey tasted like molten gold, but it didn't lift his dark mood. He turned and caught sight of himself in a mirror on the wall. He looked at his face for a long moment and then gave a rueful grin.

'You're a goddamned fool, Frank Angel,' he told his reflection. The reflection didn't reply. It probably knew that already.

The publishers hope that this book has given you enjoyable reading. Large Print Books are especially designed to be as easy to see and hold as possible. If you wish a complete list of our books please ask at your local library or write directly to:

Dales Large Print Books
Magna House, Long Preston,
Skipton, North Yorkshire.
BD23 4ND